Spacebean

Jo Harbour

Kindle Direct Publishing

To the people who said I can't, I absolutely can, here's proof.
To the people who said I can, turns out you're right.

Many thanks to my Husband, Grant, my Oldest Friend, Lesley, and my
Mother. You all are the best editors I could ask for, especially without a
budget.

Last but not least, I have to thank my cat, she devoured
my manuscript, almost literally, and she's the inspiration
for someone you are about to meet.

CONTENTS

CHAPTER 1

If one more drop of who-knows-what falls in my eye…
"AAAARRRGGGH!!!" The clunk of my friend's brown cowboy boots
followed by the graceful tapping of my sister's pink kitten heels
heralds company. Two faces appear. Kara's perfect, heart shaped,
porcelain face with bright blue eyes framed with long dark lashes
and a cupid's bow mouth showed concern. Sheridan, however,
was biting her full lips to suppress the laugh sparkling in her
dark brown eyes. They were a study in contrasts, Kara tall, pale,
and willowy; Sheridan short, sturdily built, with deep brown skin.
"What the f…" overlaps with "Stacea, are you…" A snarl from
Flossie drowns out both women. "I'm fine, just this blasted leak in
the atmo-sensor line…again" grabbing a clean towel, I wipe what I
hope is just condensation out of my eye and crawl out from under
the tangle of tubes and wire beneath the console of Carol, my ship.
She looks like a kidney bean, but she's served me well since Kara
and I's parents died a few years ago. She might look less like a bean
if she weren't painted a dull red, but shiny ships draw the wrong
kind of attention, I don't do pleasure travel or thrill runs. Our
parents were scientists with the Coalition, both of us were born on
Earth while our parents were stationed there. Once we were older,
our parents moved to a space station with a good school, and we
stayed until Kara graduated. Shortly after, our parents suffered
a fatal ship crash, they left enough money to give us a fighting
chance out here. We went into the delivery business, brought my
best friend Sheridan along, and have done well ever since. It's
safe, it pays, and I can do plenty of business that's legal and above
board. Sure smuggling, tourism, or thrill runs pay better, but

the overhead would be a nightmare. There's additional insurance, bribes, luxury upgrades, speed upgrades...

"...going to have to sell foot photos on the interwebz if we don't pick up something soon"

"What?!"

Rolling her eyes, Sheridan repeated "I said, we're all going to have to start a sketchy side hustle if we don't pick up a delivery soon"

"Sorry, I was woolgathering, we aren't in danger of selling our soles just yet" Nobody laughs. "Soles? Get it? Because feet..." Kara reluctantly chuckles, "You definitely got your sense of humor from Dad." My sense of humor wasn't the only thing I got from our father. While Kara has our mother's willowy grace and refined beauty, I am shorter, rounder, brunette, and freckled like our father, with gray eyes framed with short lashes. The only thing that marks Kara and I as sisters are our identical brows, nose, and chin. "Well, I thought it was funny, I'll check the boards later and see what's available"

While we are in good shape, we do need to find our next shipping commission before too long. Perhaps something with multiple stops, or at least a good bit of distance. Our more recent jobs have been short runs and boring, we could all use an adventure, or at least something nearer to a vacation. My thoughts were interrupted by a ding from the comm-unit, "Inspector Oren Colvin, requesting entry."

"Wonder what he wants?" Sheridan's voice drips with sarcasm.

"To deliver a list of faults and fine us into the ground, the conniving little weasel, if he doesn't lay off I have have a mind to take his face and show him where he's got the stick stuck" Kara finished with a fairly crude gesture that made it clear where she meant. "Well Kara, I got dad's sense of humor, and apparently you got mom's sense of violence." With a collective groan, we head to the large cargo hatch to greet the human equivalent of a rulebook.

As the ramp hits the ground, his black boots, polished to a regulation shine, march into the cargo bay. His annoyingly regulation voice cuts through the space "Anything to declare, Ms Thrush? Also, don't forget that you'll need to submit manifests and an itinerary for your next trip prior to taking off again." How does he even know this stuff? I haven't picked up a run yet. He taps his regulation pen on his ever present regulation clipboard, ready to ticket me at the first opportunity. His starched black uniform, regulation spotless. Flossie, the traitorous wretch, weaves around his feet, leaving stray aqua hairs on his pant leg. I have to fight the laugh that threatens to escape at the mess she's leaving, for some reason she absolutely adores the inspector, and she is alone in that sentiment. He doesn't acknowledge her immediately, and I secretly hope she'll try to climb his body for attention and leave claw marks on his perfectly shined boots. As he finally leans down to scratch her head, I ponder my response to this regulation nuisance. Sometimes I'm flippant, others I am downright rude. I know I shouldn't be, but really, ruffling his neatly organized feathers is just too much fun. I choose flippant, flippant won't get me fined into oblivion…probably. "Well, Oren, I must've forgotten to mention the 47 highly illegal, incredibly rare plants I'm smuggling in my panties, but other than that, nothing" I swear even his regulation cropped black hair vibrated with irritation at my obnoxious statement. "No Oren, nothing yet, and I'll be sure the paperwork is in order for our next run." He turns on his heel with a sigh and heads down the ramp, off to torture some other crew, or whatever he does in his spare time. Pausing he turns back to me, "I will be following up Ms Thrush, don't forget that manifest and itinerary" and then he disappears, on to harass his next victim. I wish them the best of luck. "I can't tell if he wants to check your panties for those plants because he wants to catch you smuggling or just because he wants in your pants" I let out a snort "Sher, there is no way that man is interested in anything that doesn't have a checklist, a schedule, and the proper forms, and none of that is in my panties." Sheridan laughs, "Thank goodness, that sounds pretty uncomfortable." I head back up to the control room and shimmy back under the console, hopefully once I reconnect everything we'll be good to go, and maybe I can manage it without any more whatever that was oozing onto my face.

CHAPTER 2

After finishing up my work on the atmo sensor, I shower and wash whatever goo that was off of my face. "I'm headed to the interchange to see if I can pick up some cargo or something." I shout toward the sitting area as I pick up the cleanest overshirt I can find. Well, the one with the least stains, they've been washed, but engine grease never seems to come all the way out, leaving most of my clothes with an interesting pattern of gray smudges and smears. This one only has a couple of stains on one sleeve. I've pretty much filled my wardrobe exclusively with black tanks and gray cargo pants, neither of which show grease stains too bad. My various denim and flannel work shirts are my last hope of living with more color than just fifty shades of gray. Kara and Sheridan are playing checkers. Kara in her pink sweater dress and Sher in her boots, and denim, do not suffer from the same grease related concerns I do, the occasional blood stain, but no grease. I leave them to it since I won't need an escort here on the station. It's a little different planetside, especially in some of the wilder areas, that's when my security team is necessary. But on a Coalition station, I'm perfectly safe. Plus, there's always that one annoyingly specific Coalition officer always keeping tabs on me. I'm great at the business end and keeping the ship in the air, but not so much at handling scuffles, I'm more likely to hurt myself than anyone else. Fortunately, Kara is handy with a poleax and Sheridan is the best gunslinger I've ever met. Between the two of them, cargo stays safe and so do I. We make a great team.

I stop and order supplies for our next run from the Coalition quartermaster's office, a variety of pre-cooked dishes for busy runs, some staple ingredients, and an assortment of dried veggies for cooking from scratch. Fortunately freeze dried and canned food are plentiful, stations have hydroponic systems that can grow large amounts of food. They preserve and package half for stocking ships and half for serving fresh on the station. There's no meat produced or served here, but that's usually available planet side for those who want it. Many planets have livestock type animals that are pretty tasty, and I never miss a chance to sample local cuisine. It's one of the best perks of owning a business that requires travel all over. The Galactic Coalition was actually formed before we got out here, but they welcomed humanity with open arms. In an uncharacteristic turn, humanity embraced them back and there weren't any first contact war situations. Having studied the history of humankind, I was a little surprised about that part. But, given our planet pretty much wiped itself out, we probably had to try something different to survive.

Making my way over to the large boards that make up the Coalition advert interchange, I spot Oren, lurking and watching as always. This time I ignore him, I'm not giving him the satisfaction of a reaction right now. Approaching the post-boards cluttered with ads both digital and paper alike, I scan the various listings for transports, charters, odd jobs, looking for something that fits our business. Out of the corner of my eye, I catch a flash of strawberry blond, but by the time I turn around, I don't see any redheads. I turn back toward the board and there stands Oren. I sigh loudly before I answer. "What now? If it's on the post-boards, it's most certainly legal. And I don't do illegal transport anyway" Oren eyes me like he's just waiting for me to admit my crimes, of which there are precisely none. I don't know why Flossie likes this guy, he's an absolute pain in the Brie. He is just waiting to pounce on us for forgetting to declare a paperclip or something.
"Oh there's a first time for everyone"
"Ok, that's it, what the heck is your deal? I dot every i and I cross every t and I triple check my paperwork. I don't smuggle, I don't even cheat on my taxes, What. Gives. Oren?"

"Well. I've known you and your family for a long time, or have you forgotten?"

"And?"

"And, I haven't forgotten that time you copied my project"

"Oren, that was the fifth grade"

"It was still cheating, and If you'll do that, why not other unethical things?"

"Are you serious right now?

"As a heart attack"

"Well, Oren, I'll have you know I run a CLEAN ship, a CLEAN business, and CLEAN deliveries"

"But you don't own a clean shirt."

"Seriously?!?" I spin to leave and walk smack into that strawberry blonde I spotted earlier.

I grasp his arms to steady myself and, whoa, muscles. Muscles wrapped in soft cotton that smells like sunshine. His broad chest is covered in a white shirt with no stains, unlike my black tank and stained denim work shirt. I look up into a clean shaven face with a scattering of freckles, bright blue eyes with long lashes that turn a light gold at the tip, topped by curly reddish blond hair, pulled into a low ponytail. The man is literally the definition of handsome in a boyish but also rugged kind of way. Also, I've been standing here holding his arms for way longer than strictly necessary.

"I'm so sor…" I start.

"Are you ok?" he says at the same time.

Dimples, the man has dimples. At this point I realize I'm staring, but I just can't help it. Oh, crap, he asked me a question. "I'm fine, are you fine? You look fine, and I mean like, FINE fine, oh, or umm…." Well, I'm a genius. Fortunately strawberry blond dimples chuckles and I realize I'm still holding his arms. I let go abruptly, with just a tiny pang of regret. "I believe I overheard something about a shipping business? You may be exactly what I need." Oh Gouda, I hope so. Where did that thought come from? I have got to stop getting lost in my head like this, Dimples is going to think I'm crazy. Frankly, he's probably not wrong at this point.

I slowly turn to Mr. Can't-Let-It-Go, "Well, it seems I have perfectly legal and above board business to discuss with this, um, Mr, um…" "Finn, Finn Nivalia" Even his name is warm and friendly. Like his smile, and his eyes, and his ar…alright already. Business. "With Finn here, so if you'll just excuse us, we'll be going anywhere you aren't to hash out the particulars of our business exchange. So if you don't mind? I'll be getting the documents submitted in a timely manner. Like. I. Always. Do. to the proper office, thank-you-very-much" With that I turned, grabbed Finn's arm, and took several steps away. "Just so you know, I wasn't kidding, this business better be above board"

"Absolutely, Miss…?" Cheese and rice, really? I'm a dolt. "Oh, sorry, Stacea Thrush, Thrush Shipping. You can call me Stacea though" I extend my hand and he takes it, "Nice to meet you Miss…er… Stacea" He didn't let go of my hand, or break eye contact. After the weirdest moment, ok, not weird, more like breathless… I finally let go and we settle into seats at a table in a nearby sitting area.

"So about this cargo"

"Right, yes, the cargo. It's sealed in a special container, due to fragility, it's several old-Earth vegetables, they've been cultivated on stations, but they've gone extinct on Earth and I'd like to take them back to earth and reintroduce them"

"Earth, Earth?"

"Earth Earth, I'm actually from the last Village there."

"The last village? The only place I know of on Earth with a population is the one port in Australia, and it's only got a handful of scientists studying the animals that have evolved there."

"There's actually a Village scraping by on the other side, in what was once called Murica."

"Murica? Hmm, I don't really know about anyplace there but Australia. We think that's where Flossie, my..um..pet, where she came from. My parents were stationed there for a little while, she stowed away with us when we left" I need to stop rambling. Business, Stace, business. Fortunately, Finn doesn't seem to mind. He sits, watching me talk, not looking bored, just listening.

"Anyway, back to business, I'm assuming these plants are legal and documented? They'll pass inspection? Because, Oren, er Inspector Colvin, well, you saw him in action"

"They are documented, but the container is sealed to preserve the environment and can't be opened. I do have the proper paperwork for that, however, so it shouldn't be an issue."

"Sounds good, obviously Earth is a lengthy trip. Are there any issues with making some stops along the way, or accepting other transports?"

"That's absolutely fine, the plants are good like they are and I'd love to see some other places on my way back."

"Now there's just the matter of payment"

"I'm prepared to offer this amount, I do have a bit of wiggle room, and I can pay up front" he says, sliding a piece of paper across the table. Holy Moly, no way am I turning this down.

"That's an acceptable amount, we should be ready to go in a couple of days if that works?"

"Absolutely, I'll wrap up my business and have the cargo sent over to…?"

"Carol, my ship, she's in bay SR1 of the Normandy section"

"Very well, I'll see you in two days"

We both stand but neither of us moves. I reach out my hand again, one more shake of his warm hand may be excessive but, who cares? He takes my hand and grasps it in both of his.

"Miss Thrush, I very much look forward to doing business with you." I reluctantly step away, "You as well" I turn and make my way back to the docking area and my ship. Time to reach out to some folks along our course, maybe I can snag a few transports and maximize our time.

I'll be damned if I hadn't made it three steps before Oren was walking next to me.

"What?" I swear, he can't stay out of my business.

"Nothing, looks like you found some business. I'll be making a thorough inspection."

"Of course you will"

"I'll also need copies of all of the documentation for his sealed cargo"

I stopped and turned, "Were you seriously eavesdropping?"

Oren turned abruptly down a hallway. With a huff, I turned and headed to the ship. That weasel is not going to ruin our next run, or I'll feed him to Flossie. Except she won't eat him, she adores him. The brat.

CHAPTER 3

I walk into the dome shaped bridge of my ship to find my sister and friend pouring over a list of supplies. "I have good news! Not only do we have a long run, it's the type that will allow for multiple stops. Also the client is kind of a hunk and I know that's not essential, but, it's a bonus"

Sheridan snorts, "I don't care what he looks like as long as the money is good, right Kara?"

"Yeah, sisters before misters and all that, so where are we going?"

"Earth"

"Earth, Earth?" Kara and Sheridan spoke in creepy unison.

"One, never do that again, and B, yeah, Earth Earth, with some extinct plants he wants to reintroduce"

Sheridan looked suspicious "Are we sure this is legal, and above board? Why would anyone want to try and grow anything in the jungles of Australia?"

"Well, we aren't going to Australia, we are going to a village on the other side of the planet, in what used to be something called Murica"

"You know I'll be researching that before we leave, right?"

"I wouldn't have it any other way, Sher. Kara, will you check the route and see if we can pick up anything along the way? I'm going down to the cargo hold and set it up for the box and get the spare cabin ready"

"I'm on it! Any preferences?"

I stop on my way to the stairs, "Plan at least one leisure stop, if it coincides with a delivery, even better, we might as well have some fun" This is an auspicious trip, I just have a feeling.

I make my way down to the cargo hold first, the walls match the exterior dull red, and the floor is tan with various slots and fittings for tie downs. It's rather massive compared to the rest of the ship, so I've got restraints and dividers to separate cargo. I pull the paperwork out of my pocket and check the measurements of the box, it's basically a two meter cube, so I settle on floor rails and a net to keep it steady. Once those are in place, I look around, there's plenty of space for more delivery runs along the way. Honestly, I kinda could use an adventure, and this seems like a great opportunity for it. I head up the stairs, stopping at a storage locker next to them to grab fresh white linens for the guest bunk, once I top the stairs I'm a little concerned. Kara and Sheridan are exchanging furious whispers, they never fight, so I wonder what's up?

"What's up guys? Are you fighting?"

Kara jumps and spins around "Oh…"

Sheridan, a little less prone to being spooked, answers "Not exactly, we've got good news and annoying news and we were arguing over who had to tell you the second part"

"Ok, spit it out"

Kara clears her throat "We reached out to several entities along the route and we have deliveries and stops set up at Erdilay 3, Manitole, Arkensane, Yooran, a restock at a station, and a stop on the moon."

"So silks, casinos, hot springs, Yooran is someplace I've always wanted to visit, what's the fuss?"

Sheridan steps closer and takes my hands "You might want to sit down for this"

"It can't be as bad as that time we had to deliver a load of guano, what's the problem? It's not this Murica village place is it?"

Kara steps forward, paler than her usual porcelain somehow, "Look, the stops are all great and I found verification for the Murica village, it's what I found out when I was registering our itinerary."

Sheridan gulps before saying, "Don't freak out"

I look from my sister's paler-than-porcelain face to my best friend's dark skinned face set with almond eyes, rounded by terror. "What the duck is going on?!?!?!"

Kara takes a deep breath to answer, but Sheridan jumps in. "As soon as Kara sent in our itinerary is was forwarded to one Inspector Colvin"

Kara finally takes over, "I contacted one of the girls I know there, a secretary, she said anything related to Carol was to be immediately forwarded to Oren's desk"

I swallow the growl I want to let out, "Well fine, he can just see all of our check ins AND the port inspections, and there shouldn't be a problem, at least there's no way he's following us to the other arm of the galaxy"

Kara and Sheridan let out a unison sigh of relief, they have GOT to stop doing that.

"Now, the bandage has been ripped off, and it's not that bad. What do you say we do a little shopping since we'll be on Manitole and Arkensane? I'm fairly sure we have everything we'll need for Yooran, and can rent anything we don't have"

Kara, always on board for shopping, jumps in "Absolutely! Let's do it!" As she grabs Sheridan and drags her to the door. I follow behind them, making a mental note of what we will need, a few things I want, and of course our budget.

"You absolutely need it!" My bestie gushes as I stare at my reflection torn between horror and embarrassment. "I do not" I turn to Kara, hoping my sister will side with me "It's too revealing, and it's RED!" Kara makes a show of thinking and staring at me, "Sher is right, it's a necessity"

"You have got to be kidding me"

Honestly thought, aside from being flashy, it does fit well. I stare at the bathing suit and take it in. The neckline plunges, showing off the cleavage that's typically buried in practical clothes, the rest of the bodice is mesh that flows to mid thigh, and it has high waisted bottoms that I swear are reshaping my butt. It's definitely made for lounging and not swimming, although in a pinch, the mesh could be tucked into the bottoms. This is way too much thought for an impractical bathing suite. "NO way"

Kare heaves a sigh, oh no, "Stacea Elizabeth Thrush, you are buying that bathing suit or I am, either way, you're getting it"

Ugh, she just had to pull out the middle name. I look at the plain gray suit I had planned on buying, "Ok, fine, red it is" Kara cheers and hops around in a circle, Sheridan laughs at her antics and they exchange a high five. "Not you too" Sheridan shrugs, "Maybe some tasty guy will think the red looks good too?" I get dressed and we gather our items and head to pay. At least I managed to get a simple black dress. Kara's is a concoction of pink organza and Sheridan's is tight and emerald sequined, but I held out for simplicity and practicality. Manitole may offer lights and glitzy casinos, but that doesn't mean I have to dress like one.

We make our purchases, cocktail dresses for the casino planet Manitole, swimwear for Arkensane, and a few other things, including a new jacket for throwing over my work clothes for business exchanges. It's simple, gray, and covers enough of my work wear to hide the stains. I guess maybe I should look like more than a mechanic while doing business. When we get back to the ship, I'm greeted by Flossie. "Oh come here, you poor baby, I've been running around and haven't seen you all day." Flossie is about half of a meter tall, aqua in color, and looks like a fox got a little too friendly with a cat…and also, she has horns. She has huge round eyes and I've never seen another creature like her. She lets out a purr as I scratch around the base of her pink horns. "That's my girl, now, let's go put this stuff up and see about dinner" Flossie follows me, hopping on my bed to watch me put away my new clothes.

After putting away my purchases, I head into the common area to start dinner, and spot the linens I never managed to put in the passenger cabin. I grab them and Flossie follows me into the empty room. Like all of the cabins, it has gray walls, dark furniture, a single bed, and a chair and small table. My cabin is slightly larger and has a double bed. I go ahead and make the bed, hang the towels on hooks, and set out the blankets. It can get a little cold during FTL. I kneel down and look Flossie in the eyes, "Ok Flossie, we'll have a passenger, and I expect you to be nice" she lets out a warbling squeak that I really hope is an affirmative. Flossie looks like a marshmallow, but she can be a bit vicious. I stand and head for the galley, it has a decent kitchen, a table that seats four, and cabinets painted a muted orange. Dinner consists of stir-fried mixed veggies and noodles, and Sheridan and Kara volunteer to clean up. I head to the lounge area, between the galley and the bridge, and land on the lime green couch with a book. I keep a stash on board and there are book exchanges on most Coalition stations so I can rotate them out. I concentrate on the story, it's a reprint of an old, old tale, written about space before humans had made it further than the moon. A young man lives with his uncle in a desert, then some robots show up and one has a message. Laughter from the galley breaks my concentration, I look over and a water fight has broken out, I am NOT getting involved in that. I scoot further into the couch and dive back into my book, mindlessly petting Flossie, who starts to purr.

The squawking of my alarm wakes me, Flossie is across my lap, my book across my chest. I must've crashed while reading. Kara and Sheridan are stirring, I put my book away and carefully slide Flossie to the couch. The shower is calling. One more long, steamy, shower before we're limited to five minutes to compensate for Carol's smaller water exchange. The knob squeaks as I turn it on at full blast, steam rolling up from the water. Stepping into the white tiled shower, I pull the solid blue curtain closed and let the water pour over my body, savoring the heat, courtesy of being docked. I shampoo my hair and scrub at the grease stains on my arms. I hear the bathroom door pop open, "Hello?" The response is a loud yawn, definitely Sheridan. "Hey Sher, I'll be out in a sec" another yawn is the only response. Wrapping in my towel, I step out of the shower. Sheridan, not so much a morning person, groggily wanders past me and the sinks, and into the shower.

Kara passes me in the hallway, no more alert than Sheridan. She heads into the bathroom, I'll leave it to Sheridan to tell her it's occupied. Clearly, I got the best sleep last night. I throw on my usual grease stained clothes, I have to do all the pre-flight checks. Heading into the galley, I grab coffee on the way down to cargo hold. Mentally ticking off the items on my list for pre-flight, there's the cargo rigging, the engine's shielding, the power cycler, and all the life support systems. The passage to the engine is a crawl-through opening in the cargo bay, fortunately it's big enough that my squishier parts will fit through, even though it's awkward. Everything looks good, fortunately, there've been no changes since my last round of repairs. Crawling out of this thing is ungraceful at best, thank goodness nobody is ever down here to witness it.

"Hello? I'm looking for Stacea?" Crap on toast, Finn is in the cargo hold where I'm about to be birthed from the crawl-through. Well, I can't just hide in here, out I go.

"Hey, sorry, I was just doing the pre-checks" dusting my hands off, I scramble out and stand. So much for no one seeing me. I do my best to not show the embarrassment I feel. Blue eyes and dimples greet me, Finn doesn't seem bothered in the least. That's a relief. If I have to spend a whole trip tiptoeing around someone, it will be torture. I've got a thick skin, but this ship isn't big enough to completely avoid someone on a long trip. "Here is the paperwork, as promised, all stamped and official." He hands me an envelope, I'll be sure to go through it before I turn it in, wouldn't want Officer Colvin giving me any more trouble. "Great! I've got my forms and itinerary ready, I'll get these submitted and we'll be ready!" Sheridan and Kara are coming down the stairs into the cargo bay, "Oh! Let me introduce you to the rest of the crew. The willowy blond is my sister Kara, and the short one is Sheridan Reign, dear friend. I keep the ship in the air, they keep us all safe" Sheridan approaches first, and gives Finn a firm handshake. Kara nods from a distance. "It's nice to meet you ladies. I'm looking forward to our trip. Did you find some opportunities along our route?”

“I sure did! Plus a couple of leisure stops. It should be a great trip, let me show you to your cabin so you can settle in while I get this paperwork filed.” We head up the stairs from the cargo hold, “here is the kitchen and past that is the bridge, it has a large observation dome that's really something to see when we're in FTL.” We turn left and I point out the seating area and the bookshelf. “I keep a decent library, especially for longer trips.” I turn into a small hallway, “The first cabin here is mine, at the end, Kara is to the right, Sheridan is to the left, and your cabin is dead ahead.” Finn gathers his things and heads down the hall. “Sounds great! Let's do it to it!” I keep my slight face palm on the inside, our dad used to say that all the time and it drove me nuts. Although, if I'm honest with myself, I'd give a lot to hear him say it again. I still miss my parents every day. I'd better get it together and get all the paperwork in order before Inspector nosy-pants is hounding me again.

In the Coalition office, I turn in all the necessary documents and forms, triple-checking everything. Inspector Colvin will be scouring it for errors, and I aim to disappoint. I hand everything to the clerk at the desk and she double checks too. “Looks good Miss Thrush, *bon voyage!*” I thank her with a smile and head for the door. Now, I've got to scoot out of here before my forms hit Oren's desk. If I'm lucky, we'll have taken off before that happens, too…

“Ms Thrush”

Dammit too late, he's between me and the door, “Inspector Colvin”

“All your papers are in order?”

“Of course they are.”

“We'll see”

“Of course, now, if you don't mind, I have business to tend to” I step around him, and head for the door as quickly as possible. I don't want him delaying my trip any further. There's just no cause for it other than perhaps spite.

CHAPTER 4

Pulling out of Coalition stations will always be one of my favorite sights while flying. It's all lit up, a glowing ball of sparkles, floating in a sea of black. Once I'm clear of the docking zone, I prep the engines for an FTL cruise toward our first stop. Faster than light travel is what pulled us little human beans outside of our Solar System a couple of centuries ago. For reasons unknown, at least to me, there was a massive leap in tech almost universally around then. Fortunately, I wasn't around for the wars that led up to the formation of the Coalition, but everything has stayed peaceful since. Earth became mostly uninhabitable, except for one base in Australia where I lived with my parents. Anywho, that's enough pondering our history, the FTL cruise is set for Erdilay, well, the Erdilay region. I'll have to steer to the third moon when we get there. I wander over to the common area, looks like my shipmates are all in their bunks. We won't be in the Erdilay region for a few hours, so it's book time. Diving into the climax of my book, I'm barely conscious of Flossie curling up on my lap. After joining a ne'er do well and his friend that sounds like an inhabitant of Yooran minus the dress code, the hero and his robots tried to stop some bad guy on a ventilator, lose the boy's mentor, and join with a group of rebellious folks. Now they're using tiny ships to take down a space station. I'm so intent on what's happening, that I don't notice Finn coming in, what I do notice is Flossie. The growl that started in her chest and gradually becomes louder, until it's a full blown snarl. I look up from my book, her fangs are extending and she tenses to pounce, "Flossie, no!" A startled Finn turns in time to avoid her pounce, "Well, kitty, seems we haven't met yet..." A snarl and a hiss from Flossie cuts him off, I bound off the couch, grab her mid pounce, and hurriedly shove her in my quarters. "Sorry about that, I don't know what got into her, she's normally friendly"

"Oh, no worries, I'm sure it'll just take her some time to warm up to me"

"Probably so, is your cabin to your liking?"

"It is, thank you for the extra blanket"

"FTL gets a bit chilly, if you don't mind, I need to check in on our heading"

Finn picks up the tea he'd been preparing, "Mind if I join you? This is the smallest ship I've been on, I don't usually see anything but a passenger bunk"

"Sure, I'll give you the grand tour of Carol, you've seen the cargo bay, the galley and common area, the rooms are identical, all that's left is the bubble where comms and controls are, tada!"

I spread my arms and like I've really shown him something "That's about all there is to her"

"I can tell she's well kept and reliable"

"Oh absolutely, she's my baby and she's big enough to keep us in business but not so big she's a financial drain"

"And you are her sole mechanic?"

"Yes Siree! I've always had a knack for it."

"Impressive" We wander into the hub of the ship and I pull up sensor readings to check our heading, location, and for any nearby vessels. Everything looks good except a tiny blip on the perimeter scan. Apparently we have a tag-along, it looks like a single person craft, nothing to worry about. "Everything seems to be right on track, I'll be taking over the steering shortly, you're welcome to hang out and watch if you'd like?"

Finn sips his tea, "Oh absolutely, just tell me if I get underfoot"

Concentrating on the controls, I begin the sequence to pull out of FTL so I could steer us to Erdilay 3, the textile manufacturing moon. "Are you familiar with Erdilay?" my eyes never leave the controls, but I could do this in my sleep if I could see through my eyelids to the sensors. Finn takes another sip of his tea before answering. "I know that most of the silk in the galaxy comes from

here, but that's about the extent of my knowledge"
"The planet is a dense jungle inhabited by silkworms that could swallow a man whole, they aren't very friendly, either. Harvesters work from the nearest moon, ship the silk fibers to the second moon where it's processed and woven." Finn surprises me by following up "So we are going to 3 to pick up finished goods?"
"Correct, two orders, aerial silks for performers on Manitole and robes for the largest hot spring resort on Arkensane" The blip I'd seen during FTL was still tailing us, gonna have to look into that further. The ship slides into the port at Erdilay 3 and the airtight outer door grinds shut. The familiar woosh of pressure equalizing must've pulled Kara and Sheridan from whatever they were doing. Sheridan is the first up front "Ok, what's the plan? Double guard duty with you? Or would you prefer to leave somebody on the ship?" Kara isn't far behind her "No weapons at all on this moon, so it depends on whether Stace wants someone with her." That's Kara, always handy with information. Pondering it for a moment, I decide backup isn't necessary, "Kara, you stay here and oversee the loading, the hold will likely be pretty full. Sher, basic perimeter security is fine, I know people here, It's safe" Kara heads down to the hold to open the door, Sheridan on her heels to step outside the ship and keep an eye out. Finn clears his throat "Would you mind if I accompanied you? I haven't been here before and would like to see their operation." I know I don't need an escort, but this one is easy on the eyes and I wouldn't mind the company at all. "Sure, they wouldn't mind, especially if they think you might be any kind of interested in future business"

The meeting with the export manager went smoothly, all the documents were in place, with copies for my paperwork, the customers, and a copy had already been transmitted to the coalition office. Take that, Inspector Colvin. We shake hands with the Erdilayn salesman and take our leave, Finn looks a little surprised by this, and I asked him when we were out of earshot "Do Earthlings not shake hands?" He looked confused for a moment, then chuckled, "Honestly, with the sheen on their green skin, I was expecting cold or slimy, I was shocked when it felt like a normal handshake." I laugh as we head back to the ship.

As we approach, Kara is whispering something hurriedly to Sheridan, wonder what that's about? Sheridan scampers over to us "So, good news is, cargo is all loaded, it's a perfect fit and will be easy to unload for our drops" Well, I guess that's good, but.. "Normally when someone starts with 'the good news...' that means there's bad news" Sheridan lets out a sigh, "About that... we've had company" Kara chimes in, "The Inspector." Great, just great. "Please tell me we aren't grounded or anything?" If that nuisance messes up our schedule or eats any leisure time...I may become a criminal after all. "Nope! I shoved the paperwork in his face and he found nothing to complain about " Kara holds her hand up and the three of us share a high five. "Now, let's head into the town before we take off, there's a fantastic place that serves a bun stuffed with roasted silkworm, and I promise it's much better than it sounds"

Kara and Sheridan want to visit the shops, so Finn and I head to the little cafe, whose name I can't pronounce, but they've told me translates to something close to 'Warm Worm Slabs'. I won't be relaying this to Finn. As we sit down with our spicy sandwiches, I realize we have the chance to talk about something other than business. My cheeks flush a little and I feel a few stray butterflies. Finn takes a bite and I can tell he's analyzing the flavor. "You know, this is pretty tasty. I would not have guessed it's from a giant worm." That's a relief, nobody else will eat worms with me. "You're a good sport for letting me drag you along" Finn smiles, showing off his blinding teeth and darling dimples "Honestly I was hoping for the chance to visit some more, how did you all get started?" Pondering my answer as I chew and swallow, I pause before starting, "Kara and I grew up in a field lab on Earth, actually. Well, partially anyway. Our parents ran the research in the Australian jungle for a few years, then relocated to a station with a school when I was ten and Kara was eight. That's also where we

met Sheridan. The three of us formed a fast friendship, um, fastly"
He nods, "Funny how we grew up just around the planet from each
other" his warm smile does little to alleviate the pink I can feel
glowing in my cheeks. "I had no idea there were other humans still
living anywhere on Earth, but I'm glad to know you all made it"
his smile is contagious and I return it, is this a moment? I think
this is a moment. He sips his water and continues "I'm glad our
paths crossed eventually. Do you mind me asking how you got
into shipping?" Oh it was so a moment, his cheeks are a little pink
too, behind his freckles. "I had an aptitude for business and
machines and my sister has a knack with people and polearms.
Right after she finished school, our parents passed away in an
accident. They left us enough money to get our business off the
ground, and we drug Sheridan along with us." Finn rested his
hand over mine gently, "I'm sorry you lost them, my father is still
alive, but my mother passed away when I was very young. I
understand." After that we sat in silence, his large warm hand
covering mine. Hand holding wasn't something I had done since
school, but it was nice. Looking up, I found his blue gaze resting on
me, my cheeks heated to nearly burning. I hear a familiar laugh
and glance away to see Kara, followed by Sheridan lugging a large
bag, headed our way. I lifted my free hand to wave, and Finn
discreetly pulled his other hand away.

"Looks like you all bought out the store!" I nod to Sheridan's
overstuffed bag. "Not quite, but we did pick up a couple things."
Sheridan flings the bag over her shoulder. "We'll see you all back
on board, come on Kara, leave your sister to enjoy her worm
sandwich" Sheridan heads on down the street, Kara waves as she
takes off after her. I'm glad my sister and my best friend get along,
we make a happy little family. I look back and Finn is watching me
with an expression I can't really decipher. "So, I don't know if I've
updated you on all of our stops. We're headed to Manitole next,
the place is basically a mass of casinos, race tracks, and shows.
We've got a delivery for one of the big acts there, some sort of
aerial show. We'll get there mid afternoon, so I thought all four of

us could make an evening of it" Finn nods as he finishes chewing a bite. "That sounds like a fun evening" I finish my last bite and continue, "The casinos aren't my thing, but the shows and races are really something."
"And after Manitole?"
"Then I have a delivery on Arkensane"
"The hot spring planet?"
"Yep! And we'll spend the day there too"
"That sounds relaxing, I'm looking forward to it, but I'm also glad you've found some time to enjoy the long voyage too"

We've both finished our food and Finn takes our trays back to the counter. We stroll back to the ship in no real hurry, taking in the small town that keeps the manufacturing going. As we reach the ship, I spot a familiar figure standing near Carol, clipboard and all. "Hello, Oren." I greet the perpetual bureaucratic thorn in my side. Finn slides past me and heads onto the ship, leaving me with the Inspector. "Ms Thrush, your sister rather forcefully shoved adequate paperwork into my face earlier, but I have a few questions." Doing my best not to roll my eyes, I answer "Okay Inspector Colvin, what precisely do you need to know that isn't covered by my extensive documentation?" Colvin rustles through his clipboard and settles on a page. "Have you seen the inside of the cargo you are transporting?" I scratch my head, "Well, I checked the ropes and the robes, nothing but silk and a couple of giant illegal weapons'." This time, it was the inspector's eyes rolling. "Ms Thrush, can you be serious for a moment, please? Have you seen inside that big sealed box or not?"
"I think you're serious enough for the both of us, and that cargo hasn't been opened, but has all the proper documentation from when it was sealed" I can see the annoyance rolling off of his being in waves, but truthfully, there isn't anything to be done. I have the proper documents, and the suspicion that it's curiosity rather than the rules that are driving this line of questioning. "Very well Ms Thrush, I'll be keeping my eye on you." and with that, he turns and marches off.

Shaking my head and muttering about the inadequate vetting of the Coalition Security forces, I head in to check the cargo and prep the ship for take off. I check all of the sensors, everything looks good. I open the ship comm "Hey everybody, I'll be steering us out of here and jumping to FTL in about twenty minutes, once we hit cruising speed, we'll be in and steady for about ten hours, I suggest everyone rest up before Manitole" Navigating into open space, I set the ship for an FTL cruise. She'll stop in open space near our destination and I'll land her by hand. I step back into the commons and see that everyone has hit their bunk. I grab a book from the stash. It's another classic, this one from the twenty-first century. I have an entire series in my stash by an old author, K.M. Shea, they are retellings of even older Fairy Tales, but they never get old to me. Settling in bed with a retelling of Rumplestilskin, Flossie jumps on my bunk and curls up next to me, I guess she's forgiven me. I'm half dozing when I hear a giggle in the small hallway and a door moving. Sleep pulls me under before I give it much thought.

CHAPTER 5

Unloading and delivering the crates of silken-rope-scarf-things was a simple matter, the recipient had someone at the port ready to pick them up. There were also tickets and vouchers for various types of entertainment in the area left with hearty notes of thanks. Cargo delivered, it was time for some fun. Finn said he wanted to sight-see, I was going to tag along, but Kara declared a girls day. Kara and Sheridan drag me, along with several packages, to a salon. "What are we doing, and where the heck is my black dress?" Kara's response is a mischievous grin. Sheridan's job is obviously to distract me while Kara makes arrangements. "So, how was your lunch with Finn?" Sher asks, waggling her eyebrows. "It was fine, he liked the worms" Sheridan makes a gagging face, "Sounds like a perfect match."
"I wouldn't go that far" Fortunately, Kara is motioning us to follow her and I think we can let the lunch thing go. Apparently she signed us up for the works, which include some sort of soak, a body scrub, a facial, mani-pedi, and some level of makeover that I am not exactly clear on. "You know sis, if you didn't roll around in grease, we wouldn't have to have you scrubbed and soaked like stained laundry"
"Kara, we don't even scrub and soak the laundry, I've given up, everything is just gray now" I reply with a laugh, Sheridan chimes in "At least it matches your eyes" and we all dissolve into laughter.

After we've been scrubbed, polished, and massaged to a shine, we're wrapped in fluffy robes and shuffled over to the salon. Kara selects a bright pink polish for her nails, and sparkling burgundy for mine. I guess it'll look fine with my black dress, the one I still haven't seen since we've been here. Sheridan goes with gold, looking regal next to her deep skin tone. We chat about what we'd like to do as far as entertainment, and more importantly, where we want to eat. About the time we all settle on a nice Sushi place, our fingers and toes are clean, relaxed, moisturized, and polished. I have to admit this red is stunning. I also can't remember the last time I saw my hands and arms without grease stains. Whatever they use, I need some. Apparently our next stop is hair and makeup. Kara has arranged for the works, cut, dye, style, makeup, all of it. I'm kind of an eyeliner and lip balm girl, so I'm mentally preparing myself to look like a clown or something. It'll be fine. I look over and Sheridan's hair is being braided with extensions and beaded in shades of green and gold. Kara's already perfect blond is being rolled on large rollers. Meanwhile...some sort of strong smelling paste is being applied to my hair. Kara has forbidden me from looking until the process is complete, so I have no idea what's happening up there. We're far enough apart that conversation would have to be ridiculously loud, so I settle in and look around the salon while I'm waiting. Each station has a sink, a stand full of sterling tools, half of which I couldn't name, and a dome hanging from the ceiling for blow drying... I hope. There's also a cart of cosmetics in every color I could think of and a few I couldn't. The decor is shiny, brightly colored in pinks, yellows, and greens. It's enough to hurt the eyes, but it's also incredibly fun. The stylist turns me so that she can use the sink. She's rinsing, scrubbing, conditioning, and scrubbing more, if this keeps up, I might doze off. Once the wash is over, she begins snipping here and there, I'm not sure where because I can't see still. I tried to glimpse the hair as it fell, but a little vacuum robot was zipping around and snatching it up too quickly.

After what felt like ages, I had been scrubbed, snipped, painted, polished, and deemed finished. Walking into the waiting area, I found Kara and Sheridan waiting with two packages. Kara's blond hair flows around her bare shoulders, her pink dress with waves of sheer ruffles flows over her slim figure, making her look ethereal. Sheridan's green and gold braids are gathered and piled high, with some cascading here and there, showing off her bare shoulders. Her green sequin dress fits perfectly and stops just below her knees with a deep split on one side. "You two look amazing, and here I am still in a robe, where's my dress?" They exchange a conspiratorial look and Kara hands me the packages, "We didn't bring your black dress, we picked something a bit more daring on Erdilay 3, something we knew you wouldn't pick for yourself" I'm eyeing the package suspiciously as she hands it to me, Sher pipes up "I picked the shoes, you seriously need to wear something other than black and gray all the time." In for a penny, in for a pound, I guess. Emerging from the dressing room, I head straight for the mirror. "I don't even recognize myself" Sheridan laughs, "only because your smudges are all missing". I take in my reflection, my wavy brown hair has been cut short in the back and left longer in the front, several sections have been dyed with multiple jewel tones in the underneath layers. My eyes are smoky and lined in black and my lips are a deep burgundy. The dress Sher and Kara picked out is one shouldered, the fabric cascading down to drape and gather again at the opposite hip. The fabric is burgundy silk with multiple colors of butterflies painted in a scattered pattern that follows the way it drapes and gathers. It caresses my curves instead of hugging them, the effect is incredibly flattering. The shoes match, strappy heels with multi-colored butterflies scattered here and there along the straps. "Girls, it's beautiful" I take one more look "Now. Let's go show it off."

We meet Finn at the entrance to the restaurant, he cleans up pretty good too. He's wearing a charcoal gray suit with a narrow black tie. He's left his hair down and his curls brush his shoulders, his smile is stunning. I'm honestly a little speechless. "You look amazing" his words break me out of my trance, "You don't look bad yourself, shall we?"

CHAPTER 6

"Don't look now, but I get the feeling that highly starched fellow is following us" Finn leans in to whisper to us. I turn my head discreetly, and sure enough, at the next table, conspicuously alone, is one Inspector Colvin. "For Pete's sake! What is his problem? This cannot be about that science project ages ago!" I excuse myself and step over to his table "What the cold nethers of space is your problem?" He eyes me over the menu for a second. I can't tell what he's thinking, but it probably has to do with either fabric starch or regulations. "Nice dress" Ok, I'm mildly dumbfounded, as he continues "It would be a shame if you had to wear it in a cell someplace" and there's the Oren I know and loathe. "You are more than welcome to inspect my cargo and paperwork again, although it will have to wait until later, because I happen to have plans" I place my hands on my hips and Oren rolled his eyes, "I'll be there to audit everything before you take off, good evening Ms Thrush" I return to our table, determined to shake off the nuisance and enjoy my night. "Sorry about that, now, what are we doing after dinner?" The conversation flows pleasantly, we decide to visit the casino after dinner and then take in either a race or a show. After settling the bill for supper, we head to the casino floor. The gaming area is noisy, crowded, and full of flashing lights. To be honest it is a wee bit overwhelming. A warm hand lands on my back and I feel steady and reassured. "So, I'm not much of a gambler, but I have to try at least one shot at the roulette wheel" Finn had leans in close, for purely practical reasons, I'm sure. His breath tickles my neck, sending goosebumps down my arms. "Absolutely." We make our way to the nearest roulette wheel, Kara and Sheridan trailing behind. Each of us place a few modest bets, and wait to see where the ball lands. As the ball circles and bounces, we all wait with bated breath. Finally it stops, "Yes!" I jump up and down, Finn grins, Kara and Sher cheer too, it isn't much, but I won. We stick around for a couple more rounds and then move to the quieter lobby. Kara eyes the show posters "I really want to catch the acrobats, what about you all?" a show sounds nice to me, "I'm in." Sher looks at us with a slight grimace, "I was hoping to catch a few races, but if you all want to see the show…" Finn pipes up, "I'd sure enjoy the races, why don't I escort Ms Sheridan and you two enjoy the acrobats, we can meet at that little dessert shop after." It's a perfectly logical plan, so why do I hate it? "Sure! Come on Kar, let's go get good seats, we'll see you all in a bit." Saying our see-you-laters, Kara and I set off in one direction, Sher and Finn in the other.

Kara and I found seats front and nearly center. The show started, but my mind kept drifting to Finn and Sheridan. Next to me, Kara kept shifting, her foot twitching in her pink heels, making the fabric shimmer in the moving lights. I can't blame her, I can't seem to settle either. "We can probably sneak out at intermission." Kara jumps, "I just can't seem to focus, can't imagine why." The show is beautiful, the performers are talented, but I am anxious to get back together with the rest of the group. Kara apparently feels the same way. At intermission, we slip out and head for the tracks. Walking down the corridor toward the back of the casino, I spot a familiar black uniform. Of course Oren is lurking. As we stepped out the back, we meet Sheridan and Finn. "Hey! Are you guys ready for some dessert?" Sheridan looks like she enjoyed herself, and I'm not sure why that annoys me. Kara takes my arm in one of hers, and Sheridan's in the other and we set off for a patisserie we spotted on our way to dinner. Finn trails along behind as we make our way. Once we ordered, we made our way to a table, Kara snags a seat next to Sheridan, leaving me to sit next to Finn. "This is delicious" Sheridan mumbles around a mouthful of Kara's cream filled pastry, meanwhile, Kara keeps pinching berries from Sheridan's tart. I turn slightly to Finn "How is your *mille-feuille*?"

he licked a bit of cream from his lip before answering, "Delicious! How about those *macaron*?" I pick up one that is dipped in chocolate and sprinkles, "They are very tasty, especially the one with the flowers, it tastes like a garden, but not in a bad way." Once we all finish, we decide to head back to the ship. Nobody is really interested in gambling more, and the races have finished for the night. As the large cargo hatch lowers, we're greeted by Flossie, sitting and watching someone rooting through the crates of silk robes. For a moment, we all stand frozen, no one making the first move. Then Flossie stands up, walks to the black clad leg, and curls herself around it, nuzzling one very shiny, regulation boot. "Oren Fitzwilliam Colvin! What in the name of all that is cheese are you doing in my cargo?!?" Oren jumps, hitting his head on the lid of the crate, Flossie nearly climbs his leg to check on him. I don't know what's wrong with her. Finn starts forward and Flossie turns and hisses, arching her back. "It's not what it looks like" Oren says, stepping forward, "It looks like you're digging through my cargo, and Flossie is letting you, she's not getting any treats for a week" Finn steps back from Flossie, I point at her and she slinks off into the shadows of the cargo hold. Oren's face is flushed, he clears his throat "I was, erm, performing an inspection, to make sure..er, you didn't have any illegal cargo. I did say I would be checking your cargo again." Standing with my arms crossed, tapping my foot, I take a breath to buy myself a moment "My cargo was inspected at departure and landing" my hands move to my hips, waiting for a better answer. Recovering, Inspector Colvin straightens, dropping the top of the crate "I'm conducting a special investigation, the details of which are none of your business, so if you'll excuse me" and with that he walked out of the ship and passed me. "Oren" he stops, but doesn't turn, "Ms Thrush?" To his back, I say "Whatever this is you're doing, you're not going to find anything" without turning around, he continues on. Finn clears his throat "Stacea, are you ok?" I shrug "Yeah, I'm fine, he just annoys the hell out of me."

We make our way into the ship. I go to the kitchen for a glass of water, Finn leans against the counter next to me, Kara and Sheridan sit at the table. I turn to the others "So, the next leg of our trip is longer, we'll be on shower rations. Everybody, enjoy a nice long hot shower tonight, and we'll take off after." With a yawn, Sheridan shifts "Sounds like a plan, who's first?" Finn clears his throat, "If you ladies don't mind, I'll shower and get out of your way, I'm pretty beat." No one objects so he heads for the bathroom, I volunteer for the last spot, and settle on the couch with a book. Kara and Sheridan are talking quietly at the table as I dive into another classic. By the time the shower is mine, Mr Darcy has deeply offended Lizzie and Mr Bingley and Jane are feeling the first flutters of interest. I head for the shower, noticing everyone seems to have bedded down. I let the water run over me, relaxing muscles that were probably tense from all the time spent in heels. Time to wash off the makeup and shampoo my newly short hair. I savor the hot water a little longer and then wrap the towel around me. I step to the mirror over the counter and run a brush through my hair, brush my teeth, and finally put on shorts and a tank to sleep in. I head to the front of the ship. Flossie joins me and I take the controls and navigate Carol out of the Manitole docks. The lights are beautiful. I take us to open space and set us to our first jump. It'll take a couple of days to get to Arkensane. Everything looks good and I head for my bunk to catch some sleep.

CHAPTER 7

I wake up to the smell of food cooking, I follow my nose to the kitchen, and Finn is there making breakfast. "Morning, I woke early, so I thought I'd make myself useful." I let out a yawn and head for the coffee maker, I find a full pot "You are amazing." I mumble as I pour myself a cup and head for the table. Sheridan and Kara both wander out of the hall, Kara takes a long sniff "Pancakes? Mmm..." as she lands at the table. Sheridan heads to the coffee pot, like me, she's not capable of speech until coffee either. Finn brings plates and pancakes to the table and we dig in. Now that I'm halfway through my coffee, I can converse. "So, we've got about 27 hours left in this jump. I need to make some adjustments in the cargo hold, we can all just relax otherwise." With a yawn, Sheridan finally speaks "I'd like to get some target practice in, just in case." Finn looks a little nervous, so I attempt to reassure him "Well, we're passing through a rough stretch, I don't plan on stopping, so we shouldn't have any issues" Finn does not look reassured. Dang. Kara chimes in "It's really not that bad, we're small and privately owned, they tend to leave outfits like ours alone." That seemed to help. "I will help you ladies with whatever I can, just let me know." We finished our breakfast, and I went to my bunk to pull on a pair of gray cargo pants and a black tank, back to my unofficial uniform. I went up to the console and checked that our heading was still good and that we wouldn't be running into any weather. Everything looked good on the front. All of the ship indicators are glowing green, so I head down to the cargo hold. Kara and Finn had shifted the robe crates to the side to make room for our next cargo pickup and are carefully refolding the ones that Inspector Colvin had mussed during his rooting around. Finn was grinning and Kara was laughing, I felt a small pang of jealousy. I have no reason to be jealous, but the twinge is there nonetheless. Finn looks up "Ahoy Captain! I think we've managed to sort out the damage from the inspector, and Sheridan has promised me a shooting lesson! I don't know how safe shooting on the ship is though." His smile is disarming and the twinge loosens. "She'll explain it better than I can, but she uses a laser and a special target." Sher had her setup ready "Come here and I'll show you, have you ever shot before?"

"Only a shotgun, we have to handle varmints occasionally"

"Ok, so this is a bit smaller, but at least you know which end to point"

"Sure do, ma'am"

Sheridan places the gun in his hands and adjusts them, then proceeds to adjust his stance, every touch making that twinge come back. Finn squeezes the trigger, and while his shot isn't a bullseye, he did hit the target. That's better than I've ever managed. Kara bounces on the balls of her feet, cheering, I clap as well. Finn beams at me, "I hit it! Also, this system is ingenious!" Sheridan pipes up "You can credit Stace for that! She is the brilliant mind who built it." I blush as Finn looks impressed. "It's nothing, really, I just had to keep her from blowing the side out of my ship." I shrug, moving a little closer with Kara. Sheridan takes the modified laser pistol and lands several bullseyes. "I have to keep myself at peak performance, just in case." As we stand around the target, I hear a clunk coming from the opening that goes to the engines. "Well crap, that's not good, I'm going to go pull us out of FTL real quick and I'll see what it is." I sprint up the stairs and dash to the console, there's a cooling system warning light flashing red. I pull Carol out of FTL and leave her at a slow cruising speed. I run back into the cargo bay and head for the crawl through to get to the engines, three sets of eyes are tracking my progress, without saying anything. As I shimmy through the opening, I hear Finn ask if I'm ok. I turn around and poke my head out, "I am, and the ship will be, I'm pretty sure a cooling tube has popped loose" and with that, I move through the engine, looking for the culprit.

I spot a tube dangling near one of the vents, I knew it! I go to reattach it and the coupling snaps. Ugh, no, I can rig a temporary fix, but we'll have to stop at the next space station, and it's not a part of the coalition. This could get risky, but I do have amazing security with me, So I'm not worried. I crawl back out and Finn is there with his hand extended to help me stand, take it and stand, gracefully, and with no smudges anywhere on my person. Oh, who am I kidding? I take Finn's hand and I attempt to stand, my pant leg catches on cheese knows what, and I end up landing sprawled on top of him. "Are you ok? I'm so sorry!" Finn looks up at me and smiles, "I'm perfectly fine, are you ok?" The blush on my cheeks has got to be glowing. "I'm ok, you cushioned my fall, I'm not light."
"No damage here"
"Oh, good"
"But um, we might ought to get up before too long"
"Cheese on toast! I am so sorry!" I scramble up and reach out a hand to help Finn, "It's no problem really, no harm done" Why are we both a little breathless? "Oh good, and I didn't get any smudges on you?" I run my hands over his chest and then realize what I'm doing and stop. "I am smudge free, and by the way, the dress was gorgeous, but I like your regular clothes, they suit you." With my cheeks beaming like a laser I'm about to swoon, when I hear Kara clear her throat. "Um, right, so I'm going to go change our heading to the nearest space station, we should be fine to get there with the patch job, easy peasy" With that I darted up the stairs. That night when we'd all settled in, I heard movement in the hall. I peeked out of my doorway and saw Kara slip down the hall. Where in heck is she going? "Where are you going?" She mumbles "Bathroom" without stopping. It looks more like Finn's room. I'd better not think about that too hard. I drift to sleep, knowing I only have a few hours before we approach the nearest station.

Pulling into a non-Coalition space station is...an experience. Instead of the sparkling white lights of a Coalition station, this station glows a combination of reds, purples, and oranges. Instead of smooth white surfaces, they are made up of anything people can salvage. Everything is a bit grungy, but fortunately in good repair. I dock Carol, and get ready to leave the ship. "Ok, I am not familiar with this station at all, but I know I'll be safe grabbing a part. What I'm not sure of, is the cargo. So all hands on deck here, ok?" Sheridan throws up a mock salute, Kara nods, and Finn looks...squeamish? "Are you sure you'll be ok?" I give him a reassuring smile, "Absolutely, fortunately I look a little scarier than I am, and I won't be far." With that I set off. Making my way to the part shop I knew I'd find near the port, I eye several interesting characters. The man behind the counter, however, eyes me skeptically. There's just a lot of eyeing going on apparently. It also seems they don't get many female mechanics around here. "Look, do you have it or not?" He strokes his blue beard, that matches his skin perfectly. The effect is a little unsettling. "Yes, yes, but let's talk about the price." I roll my eyes, "The price is listed, I'll pay it, now." He heaves a sigh, I'm not sure what he'd wanted, but it wasn't for me to just buy the part. We complete the transaction and I start back to the docks. I'm passing by a seedy section, several taverns, and a couple of flop houses...and a brothel. Not one of the nicer ones either, this one is the type of establishment that tends to treat their workers poorly, and only collects the desperate. I spot a familiar uniformed shape, he glances furtively, we make brief eye contact, and he darts inside. What a creep. It's um, definitely not a regulation brothel, that I've just spotted the illustrious Inspector darting into. I'm going to tuck that away for later. I finally make it back to where Carol is docked.

The scene awaiting me was...not what I expected. Kara is wiping mustard yellow blood from the shiny blade of her halberd, Sheridan is recharging the cartridges for her pistols, and Finn is coming from behind the cargo looking like he'd seen things he could neither explain or unsee. "Is everyone ok? Finn? You look like you've seen a ghost." Sheridan starts to explain, "There were bandits, but your sister gutted them like fish, blood was spraying all o..." Finn gapes at me, his mouth moving like a fish's...

he's obviously having a bit of trouble communicating. He takes a couple of steps toward me and collapses, unconscious. I rush forward to check him for injuries, and there aren't any? "Did he hit his head or something?" Kara and Sheridan exchange a look, but Sher answers, "Unless he did it running behind the cargo, no. He disappeared at the first sign of trouble." I shrug out of my overshirt and roll it up and put it under his head. "So, what happened?" Sheridan puts her gun in its holster and starts again, "You hadn't been gone long when a couple of big guys stomped up and said they'd be taking the ship. I disagreed." Kara picking up the tale adds "She shot one of them, I handled the other. Got him good in the chest, fortunately for him, his heart is located elsewhere in his anatomy. They both managed to walk away." I hear Finn gasp, "There was So. Much. Blood." Apparently blood is an issue, good to know. Finn's face at first just ghostly, turns a whiter shade of pale. "Anything hurt?"
"My ego stings a bit, these ladies had it well in hand and then the bleeding started, I took off before I fainted"
"They're the two best guardians in the galaxy"
"Oh, no doubt at all"
"I'm guessing the mess on the halberd triggered the swoon?"
He's blushing. Oops. "Unfortunately, I'm afraid so." I help him sit up, "There's no shame in it, really. Are you feeling ok now?" He stands and gives me a hand up, "Much better" my hand is lingering in his, until I hear a cough from Sher. "Well, let's get everything cleaned up and get on our way." I open the locker full of cleaning supplies and grab a few things, and we set to work scrubbing up the mess.

Once everything is settled. I slither into the engine room and set to work, fortunately I pulled the old part earlier. Now I just need to slide this one in and reconnect the hose. Easy Peasy, and with minor additional smudges. I climb back out and make my way to the galley. "Sooo, you'll never guess who I saw slipping into an incredibly sketchy brothel." Sheridan looks up, "He did not!" I let out a laugh, "He in fact did. I'm going to guess there's an explanation, but frankly, it's funny either way." Kara snickers, "You're mentioning this to him the next time he sticks his nose in our business, right?" Laughter continues "I wouldn't miss it for the world!" We all dissolved into fits of giggles, drawing Finn. "Dare I ask what you all are laughing at?" I finally manage to stifle my fits of laughter enough to explain. "You know the uniformed fellow that seems to be following us?"

"The overly starched one?"

"That would be him, he has a bit of a problem with me. It stems back to our school years. He's made himself a nuisance for as long as he's been a Coalition Inspector and I've had a ship. I spotted him slipping into a rather unwholesome establishment. Granted it was likely work related, but either way it's hilarious" Finn chuckles, "Even though I don't know him, it's a funny sight to imagine. The man looks like he's got a permanent stick inserted into...um... his...spine." I continue to laugh. "Nearer to the *base* of his spine, I'd say." Even Finn chuckles. "So, I'm going to wash up while we're still docked and I can take a long shower, do we want to grab dinner?" Sheridan stands, "Naw, I'm cooking, you go scrub that gunk off and I'll get started, I'm pressing these two into service."

I step into my room and grab a soft pair of sweats and a black tank, might as well be comfy for the next day or so since we'll be stuck on the ship. I crank the hot water, peel my grimy work wear off, and step into the stream. I wish I'd bought some whatever-that-scrub-was, because the most recent smudges aren't going anywhere. At least the dust and sweat will disappear. I guess I can't stay in here forever. I wash my hair and step out, grabbing my threadbare towel. I absolutely refuse to part with the ancient thing, it's huge and I love it. I dry off, dress, and head back to the galley, following the smell of pasta, tomato sauce, and tons of garlic. "Mmmm, Spaghetti?" Kara is pulling breadsticks out of the small oven, "Yep!" I slide into the chair next to Finn, Flossie wraps herself around my leg, I could swear she's trying to keep extra space between us. Sheridan brings plates to the table, Kara sets the breadsticks down and joins Finn and I while Sher goes back for the pot of pasta. "Here it is, Mom's spaghetti!" There's little conversation as we fill first our plates, then our mouths. It's a comfortable silence, we're all absorbed in the delicious food for several minutes. "Every time, this is just the best, I just have to focus on the food." Finn nods and continues eating, Sher and Kara nod and continue eating. Once we've emptied our plates, conversation starts back up. "Sheridan, this is outstanding. Tomatoes have been in short supply back home, it's actually one of the species I'm trying to reestablish." Sher answers him with a grin "I can give you my recipe, it won't turn out quite like this, but it's still good"

"That would be great! I sure hope I can do it justice."

"I'm sure you'll do just fine."

I yawn, sort of interrupting their chat. "I'll help with cleanup, then I'm off to get us back on our way and get some rest." Finn stands, "I'll take care of cleanup if you want to get us going and then head for bed." I couldn't possibly let him...or could I? I hate doing dishes. "If you don't mind, I really am pretty bushed." Finn took my plate with a grin, "You ladies go on about your business, I've got this." I'm not arguing with an offer that good. I head for the console and pilot us out of the docking zone. I take another moment to admire the pink glow of the station before I point us into the dark of space. The next FTL run will be a bit long, but the destination? Definitely worth it. With everything set, I make my way to bed, Flossie is already curled up and snoring.

I'm not sure why I'm awake, but I hear movement and a soft chuckle. That's not Kara. I step to the door in time to see Sheridan slipping down the hall. What the-absolute-cheddar-cheese is going on? First Kara, now Sheridan, and I've been trying to ignore it, but all while Finn has been flirting with me? Excuse me, no way in the veiny-moldy-Gorgonzola is this ok. When did I start using cheese as an expletive? What does it matter? I'm definitely not going back to sleep, but confrontation isn't my style either, so I guess I'll be sitting here fuming until breakfast.

CHAPTER 8

I smell…pancakes? I stretch and get up, following my nose to the galley. I lay eyes on Sheridan and Kara and it all comes back. I've heard and seen both of them slipping into the hall at night. Sulking may not be the most mature option, but it's happening. I sit at the table glaring. Meanwhile my sister and my best friend continue carrying on as if everything is fine. I guess they don't know their…speak of the two-timing, maybe three-timing, bastard. Finn wanders into the kitchen sleepily and before I know what I'm doing, I hurl a pancake at his head. For being more or less harmless, apparently I'm a good shot with a pancake. It slides down his face and falls to the floor. Flossie prances over, takes in her teeth, and retreats to the corner, where she devours it. Silence drags on. I don't know what to say, but at least I'm not the only speechless one. There's a ding from the comm unit, "Inspector Oren Colvin is directing you to pull out of FTL immediately and await his approach." Great, that's definitely what we need in the middle of this. I get up and go to the controls, pulling us out of FTL, and we all wait in silence for the Inspector to join us. As soon as the airlock opens, Flossie makes a beeline for Oren, weaving around his legs as he stalks straight for me. He grabs my arms and looks me over, I'm not sure what's gotten into him. "Can I help you?" he quickly drops his hands, his expression all business again. "I'm here to follow up on the attempted robbery of your ship, I'll just take your statement and you can be on your way."

"Just like that? Huh"

"Excuse me? The coalition takes all attacks seriously."

"But why you? Also, we're obviously fine"

"I can see that"

"Well, I wasn't here when it happened, you'll be needing to speak with my passenger and crew, and I'll be needing to go inspect my engine" Was that a hint of relief in his expression? Weird.

I make my way down to the cargo bay. I don't need to check the engine, not really, I just needed to escape. I have no idea what's going on, not with anyone on my ship. I'm not even sure how I feel about it. I've flirted with Finn, I like him too. His bright blue eyes, his curls and freckles. He's so charming too. But if he's sneaking around with Kara AND Sheridan, he's definitely not relationship material. Do I even want a relationship? Also...why isn't he sneaking into my room? Is it because I'm not attractive? Before my train of thought stops at that station, I hear footsteps coming down, I turn and it's Finn. "The inspector took my very brief statement, since I was, erm, not very involved." I glare at him as he approaches. "So, the pancake, mind if I ask what I did? Because you had some serious aim and force going on."
"Are you serious? Do you think I'm stupid?"
"Yes to the first, as to the second, definitely not"
"Hah! Then you'd better start explaining. Why are you flirting with me, and two-timing both my sister AND my best friend? How dare you do that to either of them!"
"Wait, what?"
"You heard me! I've seen both of them sneaking to your room at night, how could you?"
"They haven't been coming to my room"
"Really, then where have they been going?"
"I have no idea, I've heard them too, although I never looked."
"So you aren't two timing them?"
"I wouldn't do that to you."
"To me? To me? Who cares about me, don't do it to them."
"I think I need to make something clear to you."
"What?"
"I'm definitely not interested in your sister OR your best friend."
"Well, why not? What's wrong with them?"
"Nothing."

"Then why aren't you interested in either of them?"
"Because."
"That is NOT an answer"
"Stacea, you asked why I've been flirting with you."
"Yeah, when you've been canoodling with my crew?"
"But I haven't been canoodling"
"Yeah, why?"
"Let's see, I'm not interested in Kara."
"But she's beautiful."
"She's not the only one"
"Sheridan is too, you're also pretty easy on the eyes."
"Thank you. Stacea, I think you're missing my point."
"I must be."
"I'm flirting with you because I am, very much, interested in you"
"I...wha..are you sure?" Before Finn can answer, however, we're interrupted by an aqua blur and the tromp of boots. Shiny coalition boots. I managed to catch Flossie mid pounce, again, I set her down, and turn to Oren. "Well?" he looks mildly flustered, "Well, I have everyone's statements. I guess I'll be on my way. If you have any further issues, please let me know." Honestly, he wasn't just being a nuisance this time, so I had no reason to be cranky. "Thank you for following up, we will call if we need anything." With a nod, Oren turned and headed up and out the airlock. We followed him up into the galley. "So, I think there may be a few conversations to be had. Finn, would you excuse us for a moment?" With a nod, he turned and went into his bunk.

"So, you two haven't been sleeping with Finn." Both of them look at me, then at each other, "Oh definitely not." said Kara. Sheridan was slightly less gleeful, "We, well, we didn't know how to tell you." I look between them, "Tell me what?" Kara and Sheridan shared a look, then Sheridan spoke. "Well, we didn't know how you would take it, and we didn't want to disrupt our crew, but, um. I'm in love with your sister." I look to Kara for confirmation. "It's true, I love Sher too. The sneaking around was us, but not with Finn." I stare at them. I let the moment drag on with a straight face. They deserved to squirm just a little for leaving me out of the loop, but honestly I am thrilled for them. "Are you two happy?" They answer with a nod. "Then I'm thrilled, and no more sneaking! That was mortifying." I embrace them both. There was a collective sigh of relief. "Well. I guess I owe Finn an apology for the pancake, and some assumptions. I think he was trying to tell me he was interested when Oren came running down the stairs." Sher grins, "I bet you're right." Kara nods. "Well, I'm not pushing it, but I hope you guys are right. Now, let's get back on course for the Hot Springs planet!"

CHAPTER 9

I take the controls to steer Carol in the docking zone of Arkensane, it's a watery planet with a single land mass. The entirety is covered in mineral springs, boasting several resorts. Our business is with the largest resort, it consists of several cabins, a hotel, and dozens of pools. The pools vary in size and temperatures, some are large and have bars and restaurants in them, others are small and walled off for privacy. The entire place smells lovely thanks to the lush foliage everywhere. It covers any unpleasant mineral scents. I land and we prepare to handle business first, then leisure.

"Is it going to fit?" Kara asks as she shoves against the giant copper colored tub. "I really hope so, they're paying us a hefty sum to deliver it to Yooran." I shove alongside Kara, Sher is pulling and steering the tub into the cargo hold. Sheridan growls and gives a good yank, "Almost in, just a little bit farther." I sure hope we can get it back out, one more shove and it's in. "Alright, now that we've taken care of business, let's have some fun!" I charge up the stairs to grab the bag I'd packed for the day, but end up running face first into a wall of muscle. My cheeks are probably beet red. "Sorry, I was just in such a hurry to get my things, I wasn't watching" I look up to see a smile spread across Finn's face, "No problem at all, no damage, right?" He's looking me over, his blue eyes are mesmerizing. I should probably answer him… "Ummm… ah..er..no, no I'm fine" Brilliant Stacea, just brilliant. "Well then, best get your things, I'm really looking forward to checking out the springs." I wander away from him with a smile. Catching my reflection in the mirror, I notice my grin is less dreamy than I thought. I look like a moron. With a sigh, I grab the bag with my terrifying bathing suit, a towel, and skin protector. Kara, Sheridan, and Finn are all waiting for me, Flossie has retreated to a corner of the cargo hold, hot springs are NOT her thing because, well, she hates the water. "Let's go! I am so ready for some relaxation." The landing area is close to the main entrance, so we're there in no time. We walk through the large gate, signs point every which way. The medium temp pools with swim up concessions in the middle, smaller hot soaking springs around the edges, and the ones that are..um… enclosed for privacy, are toward the far side from the entrance. "How about we start in the mid-temp pools and have a couple of drinks?" There's a general murmur of agreement as we check in and head for the changing rooms.

Oh. My. Gouda. I had pushed aside thoughts of my bathing suit on the way, but here I am, wrapped in red mesh, with pretty much everything out for the world to see. "It's ok, right?" Sher shakes her head, "Girl, listen, I love your sister, and she is fiiiiine, but if I weren't taken, I'd be all over you." Kara and I share a look in the mirror, I can tell she's about to lose it when I say "I can't tell if I should punch you or thank you, but you should definitely duck." Sher's face drops as she sees Kara charging toward her, looking royally peeved. Kara can't keep up the facade for long though, and scoops Sheridan up into her arms and into a twirling embrace while cracking up. "You two are disgustingly precious, let's get out there before I lose my nerve" Kara puts Sheridan down and links arms with both of us, "Come on, let's get you out there and get some rum in you so you have fun without worrying about your bathing suit" with that, she drags us both out of the changing room and toward the pools.

Finn is waiting for us by the lockers. I flinch as he turns around and freezes. I knew it. "I can't do this, I cannot do this." Kara tightens her grip on my arm. She's not going to let me not do this. "Um, hi?" Finn shakes his head a bit. "Hello." I can't meet his eyes, for one, he's wearing swim trunks, he's muscular, and his freckles continue from his face to all over his shoulders and chest. Drool. Of course the other reason is because I know he can see everything I try to hide. Fortunately he snaps out of it first. "Sorry, I'm a wee bit speechless, that suit is very flattering and I couldn't decide if telling you would be creepy." I laugh, "Telling me helps a lot, I'm terrified."

"You should only be terrified of the number of men that will be trailing behind you."

"That would be terrifying, but I bet I'm safe."

"We'll have to see. I definitely plan on following you."

"Well, follow me this way, we're grabbing drinks." With that, I head toward the largest pool here, slide in, and start toward the bar. There's no way I'm getting drunk, but I'm gonna need at least one fruity fluffy drink.

My drink is massive, it's a fishbowl full of sliced fruit soaking in rum and something creamy, maybe coconut milk. It's practically a rum soaked snack. We're all just lounging in the balmy water in the waning day, enjoying our drink-snacks, when I spot a familiar black clad shape. "You have got to be flip-flopping-kidding me!" My companions look to me, then towards the crowd. "That's not who I think it is, is it?" Kara asks. "Oh it is, it definitely is." Sheridan spots him"Why is he here?" Finn finally spots him, "Maybe he's here to relax, he certainly needs it." He's right "You're right. He certainly does, as do we. So nevermind about him, I'm about done, I think a hot soak would be great, who's with me?" Kara and Sheridan share a look, "Well, we were thinking about a couples massage and spa, but If you..." I cut her off, "Nope, absolutely not, you two go, I'll drag Finn with me, he won't mind" I turn to him to make sure, "You won't, will you?" with a blush on his freckled cheeks, he agrees "I absolutely do not mind at all." I look back at Kara and Sher, "See, no worries, go for it." I shooed them off and went back to my drink. It took some time, but I finally got all the little chunks of fruit and drained the creamy rum. I was about to see if I could take Finn's empty bowl, when he took mine. "I'll be right back and we can find a spot in one of the open hot pools" I watched him wade over and return the massive beverage containers. I wasn't intoxicated, but definitely fairly mellow. Mellow enough to notice how his muscular back had a lovely scattering of freckles. Ok, I'm convinced he's at least interested, and I think I am, but I am NOT going to sit around drooling over his freckles. Maybe a little, just this once, for a while.

We find a shaded pool with a burbling hot spring pouring into it, not a secluded couples type pool, but small. "If I could just pack this up and load it in Carol, I would." The pool is big enough to hold around eight people comfortably without anyone being smushed together. There's plenty of room for...oh, he's sitting next to me. Well, that's not bad, what's he reaching fo-uh... ok, Stacea, stay calm, it's just an arm. I am sitting very close to a freckled, muscled, easy on the eyes...man, and he just put his arm around me. I swear the temperature is near boiling. It's got to be the pool, right? "Do you think it's a little warm? I think it might be a little warm, should we.." but before I can continue, my lips are covered by Finn's. I'm still stunned enough by the time he pulls back and releases my chin, that I'm speechless. "Hush sweeting, there's no need to be so nervous. Let's just sit here and relax for a while." Relax, yes, that's a great idea. I lean into him, "You know, I could get used to this."
"Really?"
"Oh absolutely"
"You sure? You seemed a bit flustered"
"I'm de-flustered now, thanks"
"Alright"
"So about that kiss..."
"Yes?"
"That wasn't just a one time thing was it?"
"Absolutely not" and to make sure I believe him, he does it again. We are nose to nose when the splash hits us. "Oh dear, hope I'm not interrupting anything?" I almost don't recognize Oren, ahem, Inspector Colvin, in a pair of swim trunks with...are those penguins? Yes, they mostly certainly are. His swim trunks are lime

green…with penguins. He may be out of uniform, but his hair is still perfectly styled. "You certainly are" I glare at him, he grins. "Finn, right? The one with the cargo for earth, vegetables is it?" Finn is fortunately much calmer than I am, "Yes, I plan on reintroducing some long lost produce for my community" I don't like the look in Oren's eyes, "Oh yes, that's right. The Village, on the other side of the planet from any known habitation." Finn clears his throat, "That would be the one, yes." Oren looks like he's ready to interrogate someone, not like he's chilling in shorts with tiny flightless birds from ages ago. "The one where…" he doesn't get to finish, thanks to another splash. Sheridan drops in, Kara behind her. "Well look who we've found! The gang's all here, even Oren." Kara flicks a splash his way. Sheridan swallows a chuckle, "We thought it might be a good time to grab some food, I'm certainly famished after.." Finally reaching a point of composure, I interrupt, "No need to share any gory details, dinner sounds great, let's go, now." I shoot up and step toward the way out, and then remember my bathing suit. Is it too late to drown myself? Well, it's too late to do anything about it now, I make my way out and turn back to face everyone. Four sets of eyes are locked on me. Two are sparkling with contained mirth at my predicament. One looks just a bit warmer than normal. The fourth pair of eyes though…they lock with mine and I can't look away. I also can't read the expression in them. Well, this is weird. "So, what kind of food do we want, and we'd also get something for Floss or she'll murder us in our beds." I broke Oren's stare when I started talking, but a snort from him pulls my eyes back to him. "That darling creature wouldn't do such a thing, I'll take her some dinner on my way out." And we're back to speechless. "That's really not necessary" Oren chuckles, "I'd hate for anyone to get murdered in their beds, then I'd have another report to write." Is Oren being…nice? "If you insist, she loves anything with birds." Oren steps out of the pool, "It was nice to see all of you." He makes eye contact once more, then walks away. Did he mean all of us or *all of* me? You know, I'm just not going to question it. "So…what are we eating?"

We settled on the restaurant in the hotel. They serve a huge variety of food, including hard to find meat, much to Kara's delight.

"That was possibly the best steak I've ever eaten. I don't care what it was from, it was tasty!"

"Yes, babe, we know, the booze was pretty good too, huh?"

"Yes!"

Finn and I follow a little behind Kara and Sheridan. Sheridan is trying to keep my usually graceful but currently inebriated sister on her feet. Finn slips his arm around my waist, lightly pulling me closer as we walk. The night air is still balmy, but not warm enough the contact is uncomfortable. As we approach Carol, I spot a familiar dark shape walking toward a much smaller vessel. Great timing. No awkwardness. Finn pulls back slightly as Kara and Sheridan make their way onto the ship. He leans toward my ear before speaking in a low voice, "Let's give them a moment, shall we?" I turn to answer him, and our lips meet again. I'll spare you the sappy description, just know that very few kisses since the dawn of time have been sweeter. "Well, um, hmm, It's a nice night for an evening." Finn chuckles, "We can work on being less tongue tied later, but for now, may I walk you to your bunk?" Ooooh, wonder what that means? We walk through the cargo bay and up the stairs. I turn at the door of my room, not knowing what to say or expect. To my surprise and delight, Finn takes my hand, plants a kiss on it and, "Goodnight Stacea, sweet dreams and I'll see you at breakfast. I'm probably not making pancakes this time though."

"Sorry about that"

"Truly it's fine."

"Goodnight Finn"

"Goodnight Stacea"

CHAPTER 10

Our next stop is Yooran. The native species of Yooran would've been called Sasquatch or Bigfoot back in the old days of Earth. I've read some history about them appearing in forests on Earth, there was even a territory somewhere that declared a hunting season for them. I wonder what ancient humans would have thought, finding out their 'Bigfoot' was actually an extraterrestrial? Anyway, the best thing about Yooran, is that sometime in their early years of social development, the first books they found were a lost shipment of romance novels. Their entire culture is based on the Regency period of England, thanks to the stray literature. The town we are headed to is practically old London, and they'll be in the height of the Season.

"I decided to dress as the man because I thought it would be the comfier option, apparently I should've examined the options a little closer" I'm wearing breeches; Fine. I'm wearing an Undershirt AND a shirt; Fine. But now a waistcoat, coat, gloves, and hat? Ugh. Don't even get me started on the cravat. Sheridan keeps trying to adjust it. I think she may be secretly trying to strangle me for taking her girlfriend, who was my sister first, away for the day. "Really, Stace, It's not that bad. I had to put on stays and a petticoat." I roll my eyes, "Neither of those is strangling you right now though." Finn chuckles, "Stacea, you really are quite handsome." I stick my tongue out at him, "You're a beautiful woman, but were you a man, you would still be rather fetching." I heave a sigh, but barely thanks to the nuisance around my neck. "Thank you, I think." Kara looks tall and graceful in her lavender day-dress, I, however, look stuffy and trussed up like a turkey. "Could you two have dressed as sisters?" Finn asks.

"Unfortunately, custom dictates that a male handles business, so here we are. I don't even have to claim to be male, just dress like one, though." Finn shakes his head. "Well that's good, no one seeing the way those pants hug your curves would mistake you for a man." Um....in response I just quietly turn red. That's just all there is to do. Thankfully Sheridan cuts the silence, "Well, you two look properly trussed up to meet the client. Since you two are handling that, Finn and I will have a nice little chat about his intentions regarding my best friend." Kara chuckles, Finn looks worried, me? I'm terrified, but at least I get to leave.

Kara and I head down the paved sidewalk. Fortunately the people of Yooran embrace modernity where it is beneficial. Nobody dumps their chamber pots out the window, much to our delight. They also have electricity for some conveniences, although they eschew the telephone and it's subsequent iterations. The magistrate in each region did, however, have access to interplanetary communications, so orders and communication could be relayed through him. Hence our business today. Delivering one massive soaking tub from the springs on Arkensane. Once we complete our part of the business, footmen, yes, those footmen, will go to the ship to unload and deliver the tub to the household. We approach the door and I use the brass knocker. The door opens to reveal a fur covered man in hot pink livery that clashes terribly with his red fur. "May I take your card? The master and his daughter are at-home for visitors." I place a card with my name and Kara's on a silver platter in the hand of the...footman? Maybe a butler? I'm not sure how much it matters. He walks to a doorway and disappears for a brief moment, returning to tell us we will be received by the man of the house and his daughter since they are 'at home' for visits. "Thank you, my sister and I will be glad to join them." We follow the footman into the drawing room, the man of the house stands and extends his hand and I shake it firmly, "A pleasure to meet you! Please join us for tea, it will be served shortly." There are two seats available, one next to the daughter on a settee and two chairs, one of which, judging by the gray strands of fur, belonged to the Master of the house. Kara, the dog, takes a seat in the chair, leaving me to sit next to the smiling young lady. She has a fan in her golden-fur covered hand and I'm thinking I should have committed that fan signal stuff to memory. She giggles behind it and bats long gold lashes at me just over the top of her fan. I have no idea what this means, but it seems too flirtatious to be a great sign. Were my affections not occupied elsewhere, it would not necessarily be unwelcome. Crap, like 15 minutes in and I'm starting to sound like a Brontë. I realize I've been lost in my own thoughts for too long when three sets of eyes are on me. "Of course, yes..er" my darling sister chuckles, I've just agreed to something terrible. I just know it. "I was afraid it would take much more time to convince Mr Thrush, but we would of course love to attend your ball this evening." Well crap. "Yes indeed, we would love to come, but we... we will have to take the time to get properly outfitted, Sir, if we may, shall we complete our business? That way I can see that my sister is properly outfitted for the festivities." With a chuckle he stands, "If you'll join me in my study, we shall wrap up the necessities so you may both look for suitable gowns for the festivities." Thank goodness, no more cravats. "Of course sir." I gather my portion of the sale documents, he takes his receipt, "Oh, and anyone in your crew is welcome to join."

"Thank you very much sir, we shall see you this evening." We make our way back to the drawing room, the ladies are sipping tea and nibbling on little sandwiches. "Kara, I hate to pull you away, but we've been invited to a ball this evening, so we'd better be going." We exchange goodbyes and make our way back to the ship. Fortunately there's a shop that specializes in ready to wear gowns we pass along the way. Thank goodness.

"Sheridan, help, Flossie is going to eat me!"
"Answer the question and I'll call her off!"
"Please! She already stole my shoe.."
"Answer."
What on earth are we walking in on? "Flossie, down, Sheridan?

What is going on?" Sheridan turns around with a grin, "Oh we're just having a little conversation."

"About?"

"Finn's intentions" I run my hand down my face. I deeply appreciate Sheridan's protection, but I'd rather not let Flossie chew on people..she can be a bit...vicious. "Flossie, bed, Sher, you're going to have to torture Finn later, We've got shopping to do. We're going to a ball."

CHAPTER 11

"Oh you ladies look lovely!"

I release a puff of air, temporarily easing the tickle of the ostrich feather on my brocade turban, while the shopkeeper makes her final lap around us. Sheridan's beaded braids are woven together on top of her head, with green and gold ribbons that match her emerald gown with gold trim and sash. Kara is in another lavender gown, though instead of plain cotton, this one is lavender silk with a sheer overlay beaded and embroidered with off-white vines. Both of them look gorgeous, and secretly, I'm thrilled to indulge in a Regency Ball...it's just...my dress. Kara's willowy frame is easy to dress, Sher's compact muscular body... also easy to dress. Unfortunately, given my additional fluff, the choices available were...more, um, Matronly. My sister and friend looked like they'd stepped from the pages of a regency romance novel. I guess one could argue I do too, but I look more like a mother or chaperone. My gown is brocade, in a shade of puce that flatters, precisely, no one. The pattern in silver is its only saving grace, covering the dress in stars. The turban matches, including the puce-dyed feather that won't stop tickling my face. The seamstress insisted that I cover my short locks to appear to be in the height of fashion. "We should get going, or we'll be more than fashionably late" I turn from the mirror, swallowing a sigh. The seamstress shoos us out of her shop with a promise to send a footman to the ship with our clothing. Finn is waiting, wearing a deep blue jacket with gold embroidered waistcoat, with a carriage pulled by two horses, one green and one blue. I'm not sure I recall Jane Austen ever giving the horses' color, but this seems... odd. Nevermind about the horses, Finn extends a hand to help me step into the carriage, and puce gown or not, it's as magical as I could've ever hoped. After he helps Kara Sher in, he sits next to me. The ride wasn't far, and he was helping me out again.

The ballroom is beautiful, and though the chandeliers are electric, they flicker like candles. "My dear, let me reserve a dance on your card." I laugh and hold out my dance card, complete with a gold pencil attached. Finn takes it with a flourish and adds his name to two lines. "TWO dances! Why Mr Nivalia! what will people think?" Sheridan rolls her eyes, "I realize that this may be the greatest moment of your life so far, but I wonder what they'll think of two women dancing together…" Kara looks at me, but beats me to the answer, "According to our local expert on the fantasy Regency era, it won't matter, it happens sometimes, when there aren't enough males." Kara nudges me and smiles. I look across the ballroom, while most of the group is native Yoorani, other planets are represented, many come here for vacation. Like going to London for the Season. I see eyeballs pointing in my direction, "I said that out loud, didn't I?" Sheridan chuckles, "It's fine, we all know you're in hog heaven, whatever that means, ladies, present your dance cards, I demand at least one dance from each of you!" Dance cards are passed around, until everyone has at least a few dances reserved. Our hosts enter the ballroom via a grand staircase across from the entrance, in front of them is a footman dressed in their hot pink livery, fortunately unlike the poor redhe..er…furred footman from earlier, this footman's smooth gray skin didn't clash with it. "Good evening, may I present your hosts for this evening, Harold Henderson, Earl of Wenatchee, and his daughter Miss Sarah Henderson." The room fills with gentle applause and I take a moment to look around. There are plenty of humans here, although the majority of the attendees are Yoorani in as many colors as you can imagine, fur brushed to a high sheen and styled in a variety of ways. A few, like the footman, are gray-skinned representatives of the population on Manitole. There are plenty of other colors of skin, types of hair, all representing different parts of the galaxy. Lord Henderson approaches me, "May I have the honor of sharing the opening dance with you?" Well, I did NOT expect to be singled out, "Of course sir." He nods to the small orchestra and they begin playing a waltz. "I am quite glad that you all were able to attend this evening." I smile, "It was an invitation I could not pass up, I adore your culture here." Lord Henderson is lighter on his feet than I expected, and a skilled dancer, which is a mercy. I know the steps of the waltz, but this is my first opportunity to dance anywhere but alone in my room. As the music winds down, the Earl bows. "Thank you my dear, for opening the ball with me. I hope you have room still open on your dance card, it seems you've drawn a crowd of suitors." I turn to face where he's looking...there's a line. For me. I'm a bit blown away. I have about ten slots available, and I'm not sure that's enough. I guess maybe puce is my color? I hold my card out and there's a bit of a squabble, I see a gentleman with bright white fur put his name into one slot, and my card being immediately taken by a hand covered in deep brown fur, then another covered in coal black fur, hands keep reaching, some gray, some green, I even spot a human hand in the mix. Still a bit stunned, I chuckle, "Gentleman please, I'm sure there's nearly a spot for everyone, but I'll need my card back so I can keep track." A young man with blue skin steps forward, "I believe the next dance is mine, mademoiselle." He bows, extending my dance card in one hand, I slip it back onto my wrist without looking at it and take his still extended hand. The band begins to play a quadrille, and I do my best to keep up. In the motions of the dance, we spin and twirl, passing hand to hand in and out. I catch a flash of mustard yellow out of the corner of my eye, I think some poor soul might be suffering a similar non-advantageous color option situation to mine. As the dance closes, I feel a tap on my shoulder. "Yes?" I turn to find Kara standing there, "Do you mind terribly if we spend our dance near the refreshments?" Kara laughs, "Absolutely. I'm parched and tired. Although, I don't believe I drew the same amount of attention you did."

"It's the hat! I feel like an angler fish, just luring them in."

"I'm not convinced, I know you hate the color, but your dress is flattering."

I laugh, no way is that the case. We each grab a glass of punch and some type of pastry, making our way to an alcove with a bench. "So, sister of mine." Kara looks a little unnerved, "Yes?"

"How serious are things between you and my best friend?"

"Well, about that."

"Look, if one of you breaks the other's heart, I won't even know what to do."

"Oh, Stacea, no, never I, well, I want to marry Sheridan."

"And have you mentioned this to her?"

"No, not yet"

"If you're waiting for my blessing as your big sister, you absolutely have it. I love you both and if you're truly happy together, why wouldn't I?"

Kara beams at me, "Thank you so much Stace!"

"Why would I wish you anything but happiness?" Before she can answer, Sheridan and Finn materialize from the crowd. "Ok, Stace, it's your turn, and it's a polka. I know you can do it, let's go." Sheridan grabs my arm, dragging me to the dance floor. The polka is a lively dance, so there's no chance for conversation. I would love to see where my dear friend stands in relation to Kara's feelings, but I guess it will have to wait. By the time we finish the dance, I'm ready for more punch and mayhap a stroll on the terrace. There goes the vernacular again. Honestly, I would love to winter here regularly. Unfortunately my next three dances belong to a handful of strangers, and they are largely lively country dances. I'm about to wilt when I realize my next dance is with Finn. Surely he'll show me some mercy. Sure enough, he's waiting at the edge of the dance floor with refreshment in hand. "You look like you need a break. Let's go for a stroll on the terrace or through the garden, milady" I take his proffered arm with a sigh of relief, "thank goodness, this brocade doesn't breathe."

"Well, it looks lovely on you."

"Thank you. Sorry to wimp out on the dance."

"I'd just as soon talk with you. I am not disappointed." The gold in his hair is highlighted by the lanterns on the terrace, he's left it loose and it suits him, even if it's less than fashionable.I reach to touch it, tucking a bit behind his ear. It seems very…intimate. He turns slightly and presses a kiss to my palm. Jane Austen never prepared me for this, thank goodness for Julia Quinn. I'm not sure how long we've been out here, but a cleared throat pulls my attention. It's the unfortunate soul in the mustard yellow outfit, his face cast in shadow but his form a bit familiar. He extends a hand, "Sorry to interrupt, but our waltz is about to start." I turn and smile at Finn as I move toward mustard man. "I'll see you for our second dance later." I take the offered arm without glancing at my partner's face. "I'm terribly sorry, but we are about to be quite a spectacle between your mustard and my puce." I hear a chuckle and he's twirling me to face him as we step into the waltz. "What the havarti are you doing?!?"

"Why are you replacing swear words with cheese? You know it's the same thing as just saying it."

"Thanks for quoting our sixth grade teacher Oren."

"Sorry, I can't help myself. As to what I'm doing…I'm waltzing with you."

"Why?"

"Because I put on this atrocious suit and came to this ball to keep an eye on you, what if the bandits followed you all? I wanted to check up on you."

"Now THAT I believe. You're always checking up on me. I really don't need a babysitter."

"If you'd stay away from trouble, I wouldn't always be on your case."

"Are we back at that science fair project?"

"It was history, and no, I'm referring to the bandits"

"I didn't invite them, plus Kara and Sher would NEVER let anything happen to me." Fortunately our dance is drawing to an end. Oren bows over my hand and turns and walks away.

I didn't see any mustard yellow for the rest of the ball, and fortunately the final waltz was my second dance with Finn. I let the glow it gave me follow us as we head to the ship. "Well, I say we spend tonight here, shower while we're still planet side, and leave in the morning."

"Sounds like a plan."

Sher looked a bit...off. "Stace, can I borrow you a minute? I want you to see something."

"Sure, what's up?"

She waited for Kara and Finn to head into Carol. "I know this may be very weird for you, but I bought your sister an engagement ring, I just, with your parents gone and all, I didn't know, um well..."

"Are you asking for my blessing to propose to my sister?"

"Yes"

"Do it. I would be thrilled for you to fully be family and I think you two are very good for each other."

"Do you think she'll want to?"

"I think your odds are pretty good" Sher throws her arms around me, "Thank you! I want to wait until the time is right, and I got her this." She opens a ring box to show me the ring. It's beautiful and just Kara's taste. "I think she'll love it."

We all slept late the next morning, and as I finally drag myself out of bed, I heard a knock coming from outside. I stepped out of the cargo hold and found an entire troupe of what I really hope are performers of some sort, otherwise, we might be in danger.

CHAPTER 12

Fortunately, my guess was good, they are an acting troupe. Apparently their ship is at a nearby station for repairs and they need a lift. "It's only fair to tell you that the cargo hold is all the space I have, it is climate controlled, so it's not bad, but the floor is hard." The leader grins, "We do not mind at all, but yours is the only ship stopping at the station that we need to go to for days, so if we had to sleep on rocks, we would make do." This guy is a wee bit dramatic, but theater folks are theater folks I guess. "As a bonus, we will offer you a command performance from our repertoire. Would you prefer a comedy? A tragedy? Or perhaps both?" I ponder for a moment, "Good sir, show us what you will." Ok, definitely time to depart from Yooran, it's soaked into my brain. I head up to do my pre-flight checks as the actors huddle together to prepare. Finn wanders into the bubble where the comms and controls are, he hands me a steaming mug. "It's coffee, not tea." This man is outstanding. "Thank you, so so much." I sip my coffee while I program the coordinates for the next leg of our journey. "The actors are going to put on a show, it should last about the length of our trip. I'm kinda looking forward to it." Finn chuckles, "I'm sure it will be entertaining." I finish up the settings and we wander back to the galley, Sheridan and Kara are up and also drinking coffee. The ball was a blast, but we're all pretty tired. "So, ladies, are you ready to be entertained?" Sher rubs sleep out of her eye and looks to Kara, "Are we? Because I could definitely sleep some more." Kara's eyes are half open, "Look, I'm gonna need another cup of coffee or six before I'm pleasant company." I wonder just how late they'd stayed up. "Come on, let's head down and enjoy the show." We wander down the stairs into the cargo area, the troupe erected a backdrop and there are several boxes and stools that must be their set. We sat down with our backs leaned against Finn's crate. The leader of the troup steps forward to introduce the show, "Ladies and Gentleman" There was extra emphasis on the *man*, "We are proud to present for your entertainment, the age old story of love blooming in adversity, The Dusklight Saga: The Musical!" We all applaud. I've read these novels in the past, I'm not sure how this is going to go as a stage show. They turn off the cargo bay lights, and stage lights come on. This is going to be interesting.

Della enters and begins a song, it's largely exposition and setting up the beginning of the story. The scenery rolls behind her and it jumps to her first day of school. Edwin enters and begins to sniff her, he bursts into a ballad about how delicious she smells, but he's a vegetarian vampire, so it must be love. The next big number is called "Skin of a Killer " and the, now shirtless, Edwin is covered in a coat of glitter, singing about how his family hunts. They seem to be skipping through a good bit of the story, and before long, it's Della's birthday party from the next book. There is an ensemble number that captures the mixed feelings in the family about Della and Edwin's relationship. The Collins exit, and several men in wolf costumes enter. They perform a ballet, and one wolf sweeps Della off her feet, drawing her into the dance. This is of course Jeconiah. Edwin returns and there is another ballet, both men pulling on Della as she struggles between the two. The rest of the cast returns to the stage, creating a maelstrom that freezes as Edwin kneels before Della. Everything goes dark and the cargo bay lights come back on. "My friends, we will return soon with the conclusion of our tale." He sweeps into a deep bow and joins his actors behind the set.

"Well." I look at Finn, Sheridan, and Kara, "That was, something." Sheridan grins, stifling a giggle, "Honestly, it's incredibly entertaining, if not quite a faithful adaptation." Kara nods, and I can tell she's trying not to laugh. Finn looks at me, "So who do you think she'll choose?" I look at him a bit wide-eyed, "Do you not know this story?" Finn still looks a bit confused, "Should I?" Oh man, wait until the finale. "It's ok, I think the last half will be very moving."

It goes dark again and when the lights come up, we are viewing a wedding already in progress. The couple kisses, then they are left alone on stage. The music begins, it is a tango and their duet is about their passion for each other. At the end, they lay on the floor. Della rises alone, and pantomimes vomiting. Edwin whisks her back to the Collin home where they meet up with three of the wolves as well. Della stands between Jaconiah and Edwin and sings about dying so her child can live as she slowly wilts to the floor and dies. The lights go down but come back up quickly. Jaconiah holds a short actress who must be Nessie. "Ok, well, at least they didn't make it weird." I shoot a look at Kara and shush her. Della enters, covered in glitter to show her change. Edwin greets her with an embrace. They begin a number about living happily ever after, it seems we will be skipping the confrontation at the end. As it draws to a close, we applaud and the cast returns for a bow.

"That was so entertaining!" I congratulate the leader of the troupe. "We are so grateful for the ride and glad we could entertain you!" Congratulations are all around, and I excuse myself to go check the controls. I head to the stairs and announce that we are nearly there. Kara and Sheridan offer to help the actors strike their stage, and Finn joins me. "That was...possibly the strangest thing I've ever seen" Finn looks confused, but he's at least smiling. "The books are better...well, the books are less confusing. I thoroughly enjoyed their interpretation, but not really because it was faithful to the source material." I chuckle, and Finn steps closer, sliding his arm around my lower back. This is...nice. I lean into Finn a little as the ship transitions from FTL near our destination. "We're getting close to home, are you excited?" Finn slides his other arm around me, pulling me into an embrace. "Yes and no. But we'll talk about it more as the time comes."

CHAPTER 13

I steer into the delivery section of the docking bays, check in on the comms, and Finn and I head down to the cargo hold. The actors are picking up their containers of props, costumes, and Kara and Sheridan are opening the cargo door and helping them. "Our ship is functional again! We are so grateful for the transport here!" The leader of the troupe shakes my hand vigorously. We exchange goodbyes and wave as they load onto their very colorful ship. "Well, that was an adventure." I head back in and up the stairs to grab an overshirt, "I'm headed to order supplies, any special requests?" When I come back down the stairs, everyone is gone. I guess I get to pick whatever I want and they'll just deal with it. Making my way to the quartermasters, take in the layout of this station. Being closer to Earth means it's one of the earlier stations in existence, and it shows a bit. The colors are more muted and there are a lot more shiny surfaces than most stations. I've read about Humans expanding beyond our original corner of the galaxy, and how they believed space would look. This station has that feel of adventure and stepping out into the beyond, but also with some hints of home. I'm full of nostalgic warm fuzzies, I haven't actually been back here since moving away. I remember meeting Oren here, and attending the school on this station. I shake my head as I approach the desk at the quartermaster's. "I need to place a supply order for Carol, here's my docking card with all of our info." The clerk hands me a screen and I make selections quickly, hand it back, and thank her. "Your order will be delivered in about two hours." As I thank her again and walk away, I spot a black uniform, although this one is filled by a woman, she has red hair in a tight bun and she's...walking toward me?

"Hello, Stacea Thrush?"
"Yes ma'am? Can I help you?"
"I need to ask you some questions regarding your interaction with some ruffians in non-Coalition territory."
"The bandits on Argyle?"
"Yes ma'am, I'd like to make a full report, did they take anything?"
"Excuse me?"
"Ma'am, your full cooperation would be appreciated."
"I'm sorry, I didn't mean to give you the impression I don't want to cooperate, I'm just confused. We've all already been questioned."
"I just received the notice that you all had arrived here, I can assure you I have zero information or I wouldn't be talking to you."
"That muenster"
"I'm sorry?"
"That son of a stinking ball of Limburger"
"Ma'am, all you alright? Your reaction is becoming rather... cheesy."
"That crusty dried up camembert."
"Who's the rat ma'am?"
"Coalition Officer Oren Colvin!!!"
"Coalition Officer Colvin has been on leave for a good amount of time. Admin insisted he take some time off, pardon me for speaking out of turn, but they believed he was becoming obsessed with a specific business and thought some time off would help him unwind and regain focus."
"Let me guess, a certain shipping business?"
"Yes ma'am"
"That would be my business"
"Oh..."
"Yeah."
"Well."
"So he's been following me halfway across the galaxy, and he's become obsessed enough that the Coalition thinks he needs time off."
"That seems to be the case."
"Well fuck."

"At least we've moved on from the cheese."

"Oh we certainly have."

"So, about the bandits?"

"I was picking up a part, you'll need to speak to my crew, Kara Thrush and Sheridan Reign. I'm not sure where they've wandered off to, but I'll make sure you get to speak with them before we leave."

"Thank you, and don't worry too much about Oren. I'm sure he's harmless."

"It's not me that should be worried." With that I turn and head for the park I used to play in as a child. Maybe a walk will help me chill out before heading back.

I wandered around for a while, and now I'm standing in one of my favorite places. The waterfall isn't massive, but there are still goldfish in the pond, and several water plants that add a rainbow of color, the names of which I have forgotten. There isn't much on a station that doesn't serve a purpose and I'm sure if I dig too far I'll find out this little oasis exists because happiness increases productivity or something. But for right now, it's a little piece of calm and pleasant memories. "I just need a minute. If Oren is lucky, I won't see him again for quite some time." I sat and watched the fish for a little longer, their scales reflecting flashes of light, but now it's back to work. I brush the stray grass off of my cargo pants as I head out of the park. But I don't make it far before I run almost directly into a black uniform. Seriously?

"Oh no, huh-uh….no, no, no."

"Hey Stace, I needed to-"

"Listen you pasteurized processed cheese product, you'll stay as far from me as possible if you know what's good for you!"

"But I nee-"

"No!"

"Stacea, please, just-"

"Absolutely not. Guess what I just found out?"

"I'm afraid to ask. But I wa-"

"Nope, I don't care what you have to say."

"But-"

"No Oren, just no."

"Listen Stace, I know you don't want to-"

"I sure don't. I'm tired of the constant grilling, Oren. I haven't put one toe out of line since I copied your diorama in grade school. I am NOT a criminal."

"I know you a-"

"EVERYTHING YOU THINK YOU KNOW CAN'T BE BASED ON THAT ONE MISTAKE!"

"STACEA! Listen to me, I don't care about you copying my Johnny and the Llama's diorama, I care about-"

"They were Alpacas."

"You're right Alpacas, just-"

"Oren, no. Just stop. I found out you're on administrative leave. I know you've had all of my information forwarded to your desk. I don't know WHY you're so intent on running me down, but you have absolutely no reason. I can't imagine why you pretended to take a report on the bandits, but I will say it sure did take a while for someone to actually catch up. Now, I'm going back to my ship, checking my supplies, finding my sister and her soon to be bride, and my passenger, and then it's Bang! Zoom! Straight to the moon."

"Wait, what? Kara and Sheridan?"

"Yep, they both plan on proposing and neither one knows about the other. I can't wait to watch it unfold."

"I always wondered, how long have they been an item?"

"Honestly I have no idea, they were sneaking around because they thought I would be upset."

"That sounds like them."

"I won't tell you how I found out, it involves an assault with a pancake, and no, no one wants me arrested for it, thanks. Now, I really do need to be going."

Oren lets out a deep sigh, "Look, I know you don't want to listen to me, just...keep Kara and Sheridan close and be careful. Earth-"

"I know it's not what it used to be, see you around."

I brush past him, I feel a little bad for the guy, he looks pretty worried. Surely he knows I have the best bodyguards a girl could ask for in Kara and Sher.

By the time I make it to the ship, everyone is back and our supplies have been delivered. "Hey, did a Coalition Officer catch up with you?"
"Yeah, redhead? Tight bun?"
"That would be the one." Sheridan nods, as Kara answers, "Yep, apparently our shadow is on leave. She asked the same questions he did."
"Yeah, speaking of, I ran into him, almost literally. He told me to be careful on Earth, I told him not to worry about me." Finn slides his arm around me, "You'll be absolutely safe, I promise." He kisses my temple and pulls me close. I hear a snarl from the cargo hold, I think Floss may still hate Finn. She also didn't love our troupe of actors, she spent the whole trip under my bed. I step away from Finn and head toward the growl. She's in the corner, and she is angry. "Flossie, come here baby, I know you don't like him, but I kinda do." She pushes her head under my hand, demanding pets. I scratch behind her ears, "I've swapped out some books from the library while we're here, we've got a good size jump before the moon, I promise we'll spend plenty of time snuggled up reading." She purrs and boops her head against mine. I give her a bit more attention before I turn back to the gang, "Well, we've got supplies, we've talked to a Coalition Officer that was actually supposed to follow up, we've got a stop on the moon before we make our last run from there to earth. How about we grab dinner and showers before we go?" Sheridan makes an odd face and gestures with her head, "Sher, what's up?" She glares at me a minute before I catch on, "Oh right, I needed your help with something." I head up to the bridge and she follows, leaving Finn and Kara behind to discuss dinner plans. "Sher, you about gave yourself whiplash, what's up?" She looks down the stairs and hurries over to me, "There's this place by the Sea of Tranquility on the moon, and it's beautiful, and I think it would be the perfect place to propose to Kara, but it's kind of short notice. Help!" I shake my head and laugh, "My dear

friend, you are a mess. But I have a plan, I'll take Finn and Kara sightseeing, and arrange to meet you later, I know the spot you're talking about. I'll tell them I've sent you for a handful of parts and you'll catch up. You make all the arrangements for your proposal and we'll get there after a couple of hours. You can propose to my sister, and we'll be there to see it." Sheridan takes a deep breath and lets it out, "I knew you'd know what to do, I shoot things, but you've got all the logistics locked down tight."
"You're welcome, now let's get moving before Kara starts snooping."

After eating astronaut themed food in the gift shop cafe, we made our way back down to the ship.I could've sworn I saw a black uniform dart behind a stack of crates, but I consciously decided to not dwell on Oren and whatever was up with him. As we make our way through the hatch and into the cargo bay, Kara pokes Sheridan and pushes her toward the stairs. "You get the first shower, go on now, shoo, shoo." Sheridan rolls her eyes, but heads up the stairs, Kara turns toward Finn, "You go look at a map or something, we've got, um, woman things, to discuss." Finn lifts his hands in surrender and heads up the stairs too. Kara wheels back around, "So, I really want to propose to Sher by the sea of tranquility." I have to control my face, biting back the laugh that's about to give me away, I try to answer and cough, "Stace, what is wrong with you?" I swallow the rest of the laugh and pull myself together. "Sorry, some dust or something, you were saying you want to propose by the sea of tranquility?" Kara rolls her eyes, "Yes, before you half died. Anyway, I think I want to just ask her spontaneously, but in the right place." She looks like she might have another question, I know what it is and why she's scared to ask it. "Kara, I would be more than happy to give you mom's ring to propose." I can see the tears welling up in her eyes before she flings her arms around me. "Thank you so much, I didn't know how to ask, I know it's yours, and that you don't have much left of her, and you can say no, really." I pull back so she can see my face, "Kara, I have you, and that's the best thing she could leave me with. I also heartily approve of you and Sher. If I didn't, I'd have said no." She hugs me again. I'm pretty sure we're both sobbing now, "Thank you so much, and thank you for being the best sister ever." I pull back, wiping my eyes, "You too Kara, I mean it. We only have each other, well, plus Sher, and it's all the family I need." Kara wipes her eyes and attempts to pull herself together, "I feel the same, now if we could find someone nice for you…" Footsteps interrupt her, "Sorry to intrude but I wanted to let you know your comm unit is going nuts, it may be important." Kara smiles and then winks at me, "I'll just go check that, I'll holler if it's important." Finn moves closer to me, "Everything ok?" I sniffle again and give my eyes another wipe, "Fear not, they're happy tears. I'll fill you in on the plan, I'll probably need some help…"

After giving Finn a rundown of the bigger picture, we discussed Sher's plan. She sent an advance order to the moon for some arrangements, and now we're in a steady FTL cruise to the moon's landing station. As promised, Floss and I are curled up in my room with a novel. Everyone else is asleep, and I'm reading about an adventure shared by a group of dwarves, a wizard, and a halfling. I drift off for maybe an hour before the dinging of the comm unit wakes me. I step out and make my way into the dome that houses all of the controls. Of course it's Oren. I hit ignore, and it lights up again. I hit ignore again, and again it lights right back up. This time I open the channel long enough to tell Oren where he can go and how to get there. I silence his frequency, check our navigation info, and head back to bed.

CHAPTER 14

It's been a couple of years since we've been to the moon. Our first delivery was here, and I don't think we've been back since. The moon was one of the first things humanity tried to make habitable, we built domes big enough to hold buildings. They also added a large park dome near the sea of tranquility, complete with a boardwalk, an amusement park, and open front stands. Much like the space station nearby, it's become a bit of a historical landmark and tourist destination. I navigate Carol into the docking bay, and as we connect, my comm unit flashes again, of course it's from Oren. It's a written message, so I print it off, fold it up, and stuff it in my pocket. I will deal with it later. "Is everything alright?" Finn joins me at the controls, "Yeah, just the standard annoyance, are Kara and Sheridan ready to go?" Finn nods, "Yeah, they're both about to spontaneously combust, it's pretty amusing." I grab an over shirt I'd left up here and put it on, "Let's get going."

"So, you have the list?" Sher nods, "Yep! I do! I'll meet you guys on boardwalk in a couple of hours and we can check out the amusement park together." Kara looks a bit concerned, but she looks like she's going along with it, "You sure you want to handle all of that alone?"
"Definitely, you've got to keep those two in line and get them to the boardwalk in a timely manner."
"That I can do!" They embrace and Sheridan sets off to set up what will be the perfect proposal.

We head to the museum, it's very large and ends at the original moon landing site, which is fairly close to the boardwalk by the Sea of Tranquility. While not the only 'sea' on the moon, it's the one everyone has heard of, something that seems to go far into earth's history. We wander through multiple exhibits about the history of humanity's quest to leave the planet. Apparently it took quite a while, but once we could get beyond the solar system, we mostly left our home planet behind. "I'm very glad space travel has become more comfortable."

"No kidding! I can't imagine not having FTL, or legroom."

"Or a kitchen. I don't know that the novelty versions of 'astronaut food' are accurate, but I definitely like being able to have a real meal."

"Oh definitely, I've seen a pancake defy gravity, it was startling."

"I really am sorry, I really misread the situation, I should've asked before tossing breakfast food." Finn puts his arm around me and pulls me close, "Don't worry about it sweeting, it's definitely funny in hindsight." Kara is giving us some space, but not getting very far behind us. She's quiet and seems to be contemplative. She's going to be so surprised. "I think it's about time to head for the boardwalk, are you all ready?" Kara blushes and nods.

Sheridan has really outdone herself. Kara is still trailing behind and hasn't noticed the table surrounded by floating fairy lights, or Sheridan in a form fitting deep pink dress, her beaded braids tied in a low ponytail. I slow down, and watch Kara catch up to us. I watch her face light up as she takes in Sher's arrangements. They both freeze. Their eyes meet in a gaze that's so intimate, I have to look down, this moment is for them. Kara walks to Sheridan, and I'm not sure who's going to get their question out first.

"Sher, what is all this?"

"Kara, I need to ask you something."

"Anything."

"Kara, we were friends long before we became lovers. Your strength and beauty are impressive, but what I truly fell in love with was your heart, your soul, and your mind. I want forever with you, will you marry me?"

Sher opens the ring box she showed me previously, Kara's eyes fill with tears as takes in the tulip shaped ring. "Sheridan, I'll only marry you on one condition." Sher's breath catches, "Anything Kara." Kara opens her hand, showing Sher our mother's ring. "Marry me too?" Sheridan bursts into tears and throws her arms around Kara, I'm pretty sure Kara is sobbing too. Heck, my eyes are leaking. Sheridan pulls back and slides the tulip ring on Kara's hand. Kara opens her hand again, Sheridan looks at the ring and then at me, I nod. She reaches out so Kara can slip our mother's ring on her finger. I move closer, Finn trails a bit behind, knowing this moment isn't for him, or us. It's a family moment. "Stace, are you sure? It's your mother's ring and I know how much it means to you."

"Sheridan, I'll tell you like I told Kara, it's still in the family." Sheridan and Kara pull me into their embrace. I know we're all sobbing now. I pull back, "You two enjoy yourselves, Finn and I are going to the amusement park, you all can catch up with us later." Both agree and go sit at their table for two, where Sher has set up strawberries and champagne. I return to Finn, "Come on, let's go ride the volcano coaster, they'll catch up in a bit." We head for the amusement park, and I drag Finn to the biggest rollercoaster in the park. "So, everything here is kind of natural disaster themed. I think it was a way of coping with Earth becoming uninhabitable. Or mostly uninhabitable I guess. The climate shift affected everything, jungles and rainforests became desserts, desserts became lush jungles."

"I know our tiny corner barely made it, our ancestors took refuge in an island temple, there, the goddess sacrificed life and limb for us."

"Really?"

"Well, so the stories go."

"I never knew any of that, my parents were stationed on Australia, we heard most of it was once desert, but now it's all jungle after several tsunamis created inland lakes. Or at least that's what my parents were researching."

"My continent collapsed after a supervolcano in the western part of the continent exploded. We were outside of the ash fall, but the shockwaves caused intense storms."

"Maybe that's the volcano this ride is named after."

"Huh, maybe so." We made it to the front of the line, and are boarding the ride. "Will you hold my hand if I get scared?"

"My dear, I will hold your hand even if you aren't." We make it into our seat and the lever lowers and secures itself. A tin-like voice tells us to keep our hands and arms inside the coaster, then we're off. I hold Finn's hand tightly as we go up, down, around tight curves, and upside down not once, but twice. Then we come to an abrupt slow down before we roll back to the starting point. "That was terrifying, but definitely fun." Finn is sporting a huge grin. "It's one of my favorites. Now, do we want to ride the Tornado next? Or something a bit calmer?"

"Let's take on the Tornado!"

After the spinning tornado, we head from ride to ride, taking on earthquakes, lightning, tempests, and one tower called the gravity slammer. We make it to the last ride and run into Sheridan and Kara. "Hey you two! Shall we ride the Tunnel of Love together?" Sher looks at Kara and back at me, "Let's do it!" We get in line and wait our turn for a swan-shaped boat with four seats. We climb on board, Kara and Sher in the front, Finn and I in the back. He slides his arm around my shoulders, leans over, and presses a kiss to my temple, "Is it going to be dark?"

"That's kind of the idea"

"Hmmm, interesting" As our boat begins floating along the canal, I see Kara and Sheridan snuggle together. It's pretty dark, the tunnel is only illuminated by color changing fairy lights. Finn shifts, and I realize why when I feel his hand take my jaw and turn my face to his. He kisses me deeply and then trails kisses across my cheek. He nuzzles my ear, and pulls away slightly, I'm mildly disappointed until I hear him whisper quiet and low, "Stacea, my dear, I believe I'm falling for you." I turn and respond with a kiss. I hope he doesn't misunderstand my gesture, I'm just too overwhelmed to speak. "It's ok, Dove, I understand without words." He leans in for another kiss and honestly I can't tell you another thing about the rest of the ride, except none of us were ready for it to end. We reluctantly unload from the swan and make our way to the food stalls. "Ooooh, there are too many choices, let's just get some of everything and share?" Kara's question is answered with a round of "Yes!" So we split up and each grab a couple of items and meet back at a table. "Oh my, how many deep fried things did we find?" Kara tries to count, but I stop her, "It's easier to count the not fried, which would be the grilled pita, the roasted corn, the roasted potatoes, and the smoked cheese." Sheridan looks over the feast, "Are we going to be able to eat all of this?" Kara laughs, "Of course we are, there's four of us, and Floss will eat the leftovers." We all dig in, and before long, the table is down to just enough for Flossie's dinner, and every one of us is stuffed. "Well, we'd best head toward the ship, we won't be making the trip to Earth in FTL because, well, we'd kind of immediately slam into the planet. The first trip took a few days, but ours will be about three hours."

When we get to the ship, I feed Flossie our assortment of amusement park food. I'll have to pilot the ship the whole way, but it's not as bad as it sounds. The direct part crossing space will give me time to finish my book, five armies are headed into battle together, and even though I know how it ends, I love the tension of this part. I settle in the the seat at the helm, Flossie curls up beneath me, and I try lose myself in the story. A snarl from Floss makes me look up. Finn is headed my way with two steaming cups. Flossie hisses and slinks into the common area. "Oh dear, I don't think I'm ever going to win her over." I sip the coffee Finn handed me, "She's just very protective. She'll come around eventually."
"I sure hope so"
"Give her time."
"And maybe more funnel cake?"
"Definitely more funnel cake." I chuckle.
"I hardly know how to ask, I've, well, never really been in a

relationship before. But, well, will you be in a…thing? With me?"

"A thing?" I ask, grinning. He blushes. "Yes Finn, I'll be in a thing with you."

"Well, that was easy."

"Of course, it helps that I'm rather fond of you too."

"Really now…"

"It's true."

"Good." I check our heading and rest my hand on his leg, he takes it in his hand, twining our fingers together. "So, tell me about your vegetables."

"Well, I have turnips, corn, several varieties of squash, beans, carrots, and tomatoes. All heirloom cultivars. That's one thing we lack. We only had the resources to grow a few things hydroponically at first. We've managed to grow wheat, soybeans, and we forage several types of berry. There's also plenty of game in the area. But we've survived on the same things for so long, I wanted to be able to expand our resources."

"I can understand that, our rations in Australia were…nutritious, but also, well, awful."

"That is exactly why I'm hoping we can grow a bigger variety. There are some fields that would be perfect"

"How many people live in your village?"

"The Village has about 800 individuals. Fortunately it's plenty for genetic diversity. Although, we have welcomed several people over the years that have come from other places. Many of them actually became queens throughout my ancestry."

"That's very interesting. Are most of the occupations there related to food and handicrafts?"

"We do have scientists and entertainers, most of whom are musicians. We don't have a government, though, we have a line of direct descendants that have ruled for ages, but they are merely the final say in decisions. Everyone is allowed to have a say, sometimes votes are cast, and generally the ruler sides with the majority."

"And everyone is satisfied with that?"

"You will be surprised to see how well it works, but truthfully it's a balance of faith and fair leadership."

"Faith?"

"Yes, although it may seem quaint to an outsider, devotion to the goddess is a large part of our community."

"I would never judge a belief system for being different from my own."

"One of the things I love about you"

Before I could answer, my comm unit began screeching, an emergency bulletin was coming through. I sent it to the printer. It was, of course, from Oren.

Be very careful in the village,
Things are not as they seem.

"Well that's not cryptic at all. Wonder what he means?"

"I have no idea, we're really fairly simple and straightforward people."

"I got that impression, Oren has gone off of his rocker, I'm sure whatever he's thinking, it's the product of his loose screws." I slipped the paper into the recycling slot. Returning to the controls, I check our location. In about thirty minutes, we will be landing right on the edge of the Village lands. I haven't set foot on humanity's homeworld since I was ten, however, I've never set foot on this side of the planet. "We occupy what was once a large park, an island with several buildings that survived the storms, and of course there's Temple Island, home of the effigy of our patroness, the Goddess." He directs me to set the ship down on an old wharf. I see a few docking stations, but no ships. "Do you all not have ships at all?" I ask, slightly concerned, "Unfortunately none, but we have a decent communications array in the temple and can reach out to the nearest space stations for transport, if it's necessary. You'll find our insular community a bit quaint, I'm afraid, but warm and accepting." I land Carol, "Well, we'll just have to see, won't we?" On my way out, I spot another print message, probably from Oren, I grab it and stuff it in my pocket.

CHAPTER 15

Whatever we were expecting, it was not what we walked into.

"Um Finn?"

"Yes?"

"This welcoming party looks, well, massive."

"It's pretty much the entire population."

"All eight hundred of them?"

"Well, minus a few whose occupation won't allow them to leave."

"I take it you don't get many visitors?"

"Something like that."

"I take it the man at the front is the…what's his title?"

"We call him our Captain."

"And how does one address your Captain?"

"Well, many call him Captain, sir, or your honor, in some circumstances."

" And you?"

"Well…" Before he can finish his statement, the Captain embraces him as a greeting. "Welcome home my son! And look at these lovely ladies you have brought with you! You must introduce us!" I turn to Finn, "Let me guess, you call him Dad?" Finn looks a bit sheepish, "I do, sorry, I kept forgetting to tell you, and it didn't seem like that big of a deal."

"Um, it's kind of a big deal that you're pretty much a prince."

"I am truly sorry I didn't mention it to you. By the time I was sure of my affection, I, well.. I forgot."

"How in the name of all that is queso fresco, do you forget you're more or less royalty?"

"It never came up?"

"Ok, fair." That's about all I had time to say before I was embraced by the Captain. I see where Finn gets his looks, he's a younger version of his father. I turn to see Kara and Sheridan's reactions to all of this, but I can't find them in the crowd. I hang onto Finn's hand so I don't lose him too. We make it to a long dock, there are rowboats tied along both sides, but the one at the end is by far the largest. It's also the most ornate, sporting a carving on the front of a mermaid wearing a large spiky crown, her arms, wait no, hair, trailing along the top edge of the boat. I catch a glimpse of Kara and Sheridan stepping into another boat. I don't love it that I'm separate from them, but I'm sure we can meet up later. I trail behind Finn to the ornate boat, I should've guessed that would be our ride. He steps aboard and extends his hand to help me in, I stumble a bit as the boat rocks, but his strong arm is immediately around me, keeping me from falling as we sit on one of the benches in the boat. The Captain sits down facing us, "We will have a great feast tonight in the large lawn between the living quarters, the place was once called Ellis Island, and it was a greeting place for newcomers to this land." Is it just me or is there something a little weird about his speech patterns? "Tomorrow you must join us on Temple Island for our weekly celebration of the goddess, it is quite an experience you will not want to miss, if you leave us." I don't really like that 'if' he tossed in, "Thank you sir, I'll discuss it with my crew, we don't have any pressing engagements right now. So, with your permission of course, we could certainly stay for at least a couple of days." The Captain nodded and exchanged a look with his son. Wonder what that's about? As we get further from the dock, I notice a small dark speck in the sky, surely it's not a ship? No one has said anything about any other company. The ship reminds me that I still have a note from Oren in my pocket. I reach in and pull it out...

Stacea,
I'm ...
...will find...
...won't get away
...no esca...

The wrinkles block out part of the message, but before I can smooth it out, the wind rips the note from my hand. Honestly it's fine, I can fill in the blanks…he's coming after me, he'll find me, I won't get away from him, there's no escape from justice, blah blah blah, same as always. He's really got to get over that alpaca thing. I push thought's of Oren aside and turn to watch as we approach Ellis Island. I've never been in a boat unless the Tunnel of Love on the moon counts. The water is a bit choppy, but the two men rowing our boat seem to barely notice. Finn slides his arm around me and I'm grateful for the warmth. I'm wearing an overshirt, but the cool wind is going right through. I lean into him and I catch a grin on the Captain's face. After the brisk boat trip, I'm glad to set my feet on land. I look around for Kara and Sheridan, and fortunately they're walking toward us. "Hey! That was some ride, huh?" Sher looks a bit green around the gills, "I guess you could say that, I'm relieved to be on land." The Captain issues afew orders to the men who were rowing our boat, then turns to us, "My ladies, welcome, welcome, Finn will show you to quarters and make sure you have what you need to prepare for dinner, I look forward to seeing you there." With that he turns and walks toward the building on the far side of the lawn. I turn to Finn, "Well, I guess we'd better get ready, but our clothes are back on the ship." Finn leads us toward the building close to us, "It's fine, we have guest chambers available and wardrobes that have a large selection of sizes and styles, you should be able to find something." He takes us through a door that opens on a beautiful room with an arched ceiling. At the opposite end of the room he opens a suite that has two bedrooms, a sitting area with doors that look like they open onto a private terrace, a large bathroom, and a large freestanding wardrobe. "Well, ladies, I will leave you to it, it will be a couple of hours until dinner, so you should have plenty of time." He leans toward me and kisses my forehead before he leaves.

"Oh my goodness, you all need to see this!" Kara and I rush to the bathroom, not sure what to expect. There's a massive tub set into the floor, a shower with more shower heads than I can count, and a massive vanity with double sinks. Lining one wall is a shelf of bottles, every fragrance of soap imaginable, a variety of hair and skin products, and various cosmetics. "Ladies, if the bathroom is this great, the wardrobe probably has a door to another world entirely." I led the way out of the bathroom and to the wardrobe. It is, at least, two feet taller than me, with two very large doors made of carved wood. One door sports a lion, the other, a sharp featured woman in a large sleigh pulled by polar bears. I open the door, and take in the sight. I could almost swear this thing is bigger on the inside. Inside are clothes of various sizes, all very formal, and in any color imaginable. "I wish we'd had this selection back on Yooran, I wouldn't have been stuck in puce." I run my hand along the rows of clothes, looking for something that would do for dinner. Kara holds up a pink sheath dress, "I found something, it's incredibly soft, and my favorite color." Sheridan settles on a black cocktail dress with layers of ruffles trimmed in gold. I'm still meandering through the clothes as they head to the bathroom to bathe and get ready. I finally settle on a red halter dress with a beaded bodice and a floaty skirt with several layers of sheer fabric. Go big or go home, right? I also grab a pair of red heels with straps that tie up around the ankle, and they're my size. I close the wardrobe, and land on the couch in the sitting area to wait for my turn in the bathroom. Kara and Sher emerge in plush white bath robes, "That was glorious. It's your turn, you have about half an hour to soak, and then we're getting you ready for dinner." I look at Kara, she's nodding in agreement. I'm in trouble.

By the time someone taps on our door, all three of us are polished and styled, and we smell amazing. Kara's hair lay in perfect curls down her back, Sheridan's braids are woven into a gold scarf on top of her head, and my hair lay in soft waves. "Hello ladies, I was sent to escort you to dinner." The young man appeared to be wearing some sort of uniform, "Right this way." He leads us down a hallway and out a fairly ornate entrance. On the very flat commons between the two buildings, we see many round tables, all set for a formal dinner. On one end, a dance floor is set up with a spot for a band to the side. The opposite end has a dais with what is probably the head table, the seats are all on one side, so the people seated there look out over the round tables. Our escort leads us to the head table and indicates that there are name cards at each seat, mine is close to the center, immediately to the right of Finn. Sheridan and Kara are seated together, left of the Captain. While it's a place of honor, I'm a little uneasy about being so far from them in an unfamiliar place. "Well ladies, I guess we'll be separate for dinner." I step down to stand with them, people are arriving, sitting at the lower tables. "It'll be fine, Stace, you won't even miss us with Finn there." Ok, if my naturally suspicious friend thinks it's fine, then it's fine. More people are arriving and taking their seats, somewhere I hear the sound of a gong, weird. Then I realize it's marking the entrance of Finn and his father. Everyone stands as they approach their seats. When the Captain sits, everyone sits, and men in the same uniform as our escort earlier, begin serving food. There's roast…something, and a pastry with what appears to be berry filling, and a salad that contains flower petals, what must be field greens, and more berries. No wonder Finn wanted to introduce some new plants. It does look and smell lovely though. "Please don't mind all of the berries, before long we will have, well, things other than berries." I chew and swallow the colorful bite of salad I had just put in my mouth, "It tastes great, but I could see the same thing every day becoming a bit much." Finn smiles and nods…there are those enchanting dimples again. "So, is every meal this formal? Or is there a special occasion?" Finn leans in closely and whispers, "That's a surprise," Then in a conversational volume he adds, "We do have regular formal dinners, monthly for birthdays and anniversaries, then occasionally more for other celebrations. Other types of entertainment aren't as easy to come by." I nod as I swallow a bite of the…meat "Ah, that makes sense. So whose birthday is it?" He flashes a grin, "This is a special occasion." I wait for him to elaborate, he does not. Before I can ask, the Captain stands and taps his knife against his glass to get everyone's attention.

"Everyone, thank you for coming this evening, I would like to introduce our guests, they've brought my wayward son home." Everyone applauds, "Now hurry and finish your dinner so we can open the dance floor!" With that, he returns to his seat, the entire lawn has gone silent, everyone is intensely focused on eating. I guess when the Captain says hurry up and eat, he means it. Before too long, there are several uniformed waiters clearing the tables and people with instruments headed toward the dance floor. Now that the business of eating is done, conversations start up around the room, people are pairing up to dance as the band begins to play. That was…well…odd. I turn to Finn, "I don't know the customs here, but, can I ask you to dance? Or, should I ask you to ask me to dance?" Finn grins and chuckles, "Either way, let's head to the dance floor." He stands and holds his hand out, I place my hand in his and he pulls me toward him, right into his arms. He leans in to whisper into my ear, "Your dress looks amazing, I will be the envy of every man in the village." I smile, he leads me by the hand through the tables to the dance floor, a few other couples are there dancing too. I don't know the music, but Finn is a good dancer. The weather is lovely, there's a nice breeze caressing my shoulders, and the soft scent of something blooming nearby. "So, about that surprise," Finn looks into my eyes and continues, "Tonight is actually an engagement party." I smile, and glance around, "Who's the happy couple?" Finn twirls me and then wraps an arm around me, "Us, if you'll have me?" I. Am. Stunned. I don't know what to say, I've become very fond of Finn, but this is very sudden. It would completely change everything. My life, my business, my family? Unless Finn would travel with me. Which is possible, maybe? "You've been thinking an awful long time.." Crap, he's right. I just don't know what to say, "I'm not saying no." His eyes are locked with mine, "Why do I feel like there's a 'but' in there?" I wish I had an answer, "This..is…very sudden. I think I have my answer, but can I sleep on it? I just don't want to make a hasty decision." With a smile but a hint of sadness in his eyes he nods, "At least it's not a no. You can definitely have some time to think it over, or talk about it with Kara and Sheridan." I push up on my toe and give him a kiss, he prolongs it, and deepens it. "It is definitely not a no" He smiles and offers me his arm, "Shall we make our way back to the dance floor?" I take it, "Absolutely."

A few hours later, all three of us girls are worn out. My feet are killing me, and we are just lounging about in the sitting area of our suite. "Ladies, I need advice." Sheridan manages a thumbs up, Kara nods sleepily. "It's Finn. He wants me to marry him." At that, Kara bolted upright and Sheridan actually jumps to her feet, both speaking at the same time, "What abou…" "And there's the…" "Where would…" "….Flossie hates" "I just don't…" then they finally hit that creepy unison thing they do… "What did you say?!?!" I take a deep breath, because if I don't get this all out at once, they'll start in again. "I told him my answer isn't no, but that I needed the night. I don't know where we would live, I don't know what would become of the business, although I bet you two could handle it, and honestly, Flossie might eat him. I'm not sure. This is a massive change and I don't know what to do." With that I slump onto the chair I'd stood up from. It's silent for a moment, I let my eyes drift while the girls take in what I said and process it. I see a little movement from outside the window. Is that a..? Surely not. Kara and Sheridan have started spitballing ideas about the business, traveling occasionally, and custody of Flossie. I drift toward the window, where I think I saw movement out of sync with the breeze in the plants. I slide my finger under the translucent curtain and peek outside. I see a man slipping through the shadows, I'm not sure if he was eavesdropping or he just happened to be sneaking through the area. He's wearing a gray shirt, black cargo pants, and a hat. I could swear he looks a bit like Oren, but there's no way he'd be wearing anything but his uniform, on leave or not. I watch as he continues out of my line of sight. "Stace? Did you hear me?" I turn to face my sister, "I'm sorry, no, I thought…I thought I saw..nevermind, now, what do you all think?" They begin detailing a list of considerations, this time a little slower and not over each other. They have several good points. Do I love him? I think I do. Do I want to stay here? I don't know. Is at least part time travel an option? Probably. Will Flossie ever forgive me? I hope so. "Well ladies, I think my answer is yes." Kara looks at me intently, "I don't think you're sure." Sheridan stands and moves next to her, "I don't either, but we love you and we want you to be happy, so if Finn makes you happy, then say yes and we'll help with the rest." I threw my arms around both of them. "I love you two so much. I don't know what I would do without you." Kara chuckles, "Be set upon by bandits, I'm certain." Sheridan takes a step back, "If he hurts you, I've got a bullet with his name on it." I smile at her protective nature, "I would expect nothing less." With that, we said our goodnights, on my way to bed I could've sworn I saw Oren's silhouette pass my window although surely not. That brought to mind his cryptic message. Had he really followed me here still trying to find a way to take me down? He's been a constant in my life since we were kids, rivals in school, rivals after, all because of some silly alpaca snafu. I truly never believed he'd harm me, but that note... I shake my head, surely I'm safe enough here. With that, I head for bed. Anything else I need to do will be handled better when well rested.

CHAPTER 16

I awake to sun pouring in through the window, and birds chirping. I haven't awoken to chirping birds in ages. Even when we're docked on a planet, the local fauna tend to avoid the docking areas. I don't hear any movement from the rest of the suite. I crawl out of bed and head for the bathroom. I don't know what time one goes to the Temple Island to worship a goddess, but I might as well be ready. I stop at the wardrobe…I don't know what one wears either. Fortunately, the answer is pretty obvious when I open the doors and find a simple white cotton dress with a note that says "For the temple gathering." I grab it and continue on. I opt for a soak, the shower is amazing, but my feet still hurt a bit from dancing in heels. I wander over to the wall'o'stuff and pick out a light floral bubble bath and pour it into the tub. As it fills and froths, the scent fills the room. I sink into the tub and let my mind drift. I wonder if I actually spotted Oren lurking, or if it was a product of my imagination. Why would he follow us all the way out here? Also, oh geez, I need to answer Finn. I am pretty sure my answer is 'yes' but is 'pretty sure' enough to make all of the changes to my life worth it? I know I've never felt the butterflies I feel with Finn, with anyone else. Sitting alone in the gorgeous bathroom, I decide that I do have an answer, I will definitely marry Finn, we'll just make arrangements as they come. I grab a soft fluffy towel and dry off. I get dressed in the white dress, and head to Kara and Sheridan's door and knock. There's no answer, they must have crashed out hard. I'll let them rest and leave a note, neither one is going to be sad about missing the temple gathering…thing. I pen a note on the little pad on a table behind the couch, letting them know I left them, to rest up and maybe check on Floss. She's, well, not exactly friendly, so we left her on the ship with food and water. I step into the long large room and head toward the door that leads to the lawn where we dined and danced last night. I should be safe here, but I have that little frisson of warning, like someone is watching me. I head toward the area where the boats are docked, assuming that will be how we get to Temple Island. As I stare across the water, I hear footsteps approaching behind me and soon around. "Oh! You startled me! I was enjoying the view." Finn grins, his reddish hair glowing like flames in the early morning sun, "Me too, I couldn't take my eyes off of you." I giggle and blush, what the heck? I can be a beautiful woman glistening in the morning sunlight for once. "I, please believe me, do not want to press you for an answer, however, my father WILL ask if I have managed to win your heart. It's only fair that I warn you." I step forward and place my hand in his. "I have an answer, so I'm glad I can prepare both of us beforehand." Finn gulps, his eyes shining, but hints of nervousness are visible. I can't keep him in suspense, it hurts to watch. "I will marry you, we can figure out the next steps as they come." He wraps me in a tight embrace, reminding me of the moment we met. He still smells of sunshine. This is… nice, it's good, definitely…lovely, this is what I'm signing on for, and it's ok. I. Will. Be. Fine. Fortunately before I probe my reaction too deeply, he pulls back. "It's nearly time to begin the walk to the Temple, we can let my father know the amazing news, I'm sure he'll want to make an announcement."

"Wait, wait, wait…."

"Oh, I'm sorry, it's tradition for the Captain to…"

"No, that I get. How, precisely, are we walking to the Temple… Island?"

"Oh! There's a bridge. It's partially under water most of the time, but there's a system for raising it when we need it."

"Well, Ok, that's a new one for me. Sounds like an adventure!"

"One of the things I love about you."

I smile up at him as we set out for the bridge. It turns out there's a whole ceremony, just for the bridge raising, and then there's a procession that includes me, in a place of honor, behind the Captain and in front of Finn. By the time we reach the large building at the foot of a larger statue, it's probably noon, and while the sun is burning bright, there's a nice breeze off of the water, so it's not unpleasant. The Captain moves forward, raises his arms, and begins to speak. I just noticed he has a microphone. I haven't actually seen a ton of technology here, that's interesting. I zone back in at the right moment "...Goddess to thank for bringing a wife to my son! We will celebrate their nuptials this evening..." What?! That's quick, and Kara and Sheridan aren't here. "...we must give her time to prepare, to be made into the image of the goddess, a fitting bride..." Are they going to paint me green?! Crap, I should've asked a lot more questions. "Ladies of knife and bone, you must go to prepare the ceremonial space on the plinth of our great lady..." Knife and bone?! What in the ghost pepper jack is going on? I turn to Finn, he's smiling, this can't be too bad if he's smiling, right? I take a deep breath and then I realize everyone is staring at me and I don't know why... "Um, yes?" Finn gives me a squeeze and I don't know what I just agreed to, but I think it's ok. It'll be fine, I'm just nervous, it's just nerves, deep breaths. Every. Thing. Is. Fine. Cheddar. There's a group of women leading me away from Finn, we're headed up toward the green lady these people worship. She's very tall, wearing a spiky crown, wearing some garment made of lots of fabric. I'm not an expert on historical relics, but this one is lacking arms...please, please, please...just let them paint me green or something.

Eight women pull me into a room beneath the statue, two block the door, the others spread about the room. One picks up a mass of diaphanous green fabric, two pick up containers of makeup and come toward me. Another produces a metal spiked crown. I'm divested of my dress and my undergarments, and the women begin covering me in green. I'm filled with relief. They are just painting me green, I was right. Everything really is fine, the wedding is going to be sooner than I thought, but it's ok, Sheridan and Kara will forgive me. They dress me in the diaphanous green gown and place the crown on my head. I look very much like their 'goddess' in this getup. What I would've picked? No. But it's fine, I can't believe I overreacted before. The ladies lead me up some stairs and we step out at the very feet of the goddess. I can see the crowd below, but I don't see Finn or his Father anywhere. Maybe they're painting him green too? I have no idea, I just know that we are very far from the ground and it is NOT the same as being this high up in Carol. The women secure a gold cord to my wrists, it is heavy and sturdy, it's definitely metal of some sort, but I'm not sure what type. This is, well, odd. I guess I just wait for what comes next?

The Captain and Finn step out of a door I hadn't noticed, although it's fair to say I was kind of distracted. The Captain steps forward and begins a homily, "My dear citizens, we present to you this day two individuals wishing to unite in the sacred bond of verdant matrimony. This is a sacred vow beyond marriage between male and female servants of the goddess, her worshippers. In this ceremony, the son of the goddess incarnate will be bonded to one who will embody the goddess for the next generation of village primacy!" The crowd went wild. The Captain continues, "Let the pair be anointed and begin the march to the Circle of Transformation!" I finally manage to make eye contact with Finn, he shoots me a reassuring smile, and steps toward me. "I promise the long walk will be the worst part, the Captain will lead us to the round gathering area where the ceremony will be finalized." We begin walking down the oh, seven thousand steps, ok, maybe I'm exaggerating a bit, but it's a lot. I'm glad I have Finn's reassuring arm to hang on to as we go. I wonder if Kara and Sheridan are awake yet. I wish they were, I've got butterflies in my stomach and they aren't the good kind. They kinda feel like vicious attack butterflies, trying to stab their way out with a stabbier version of their proboscis. It's a long way down, and we're walking in silence. I don't like it, "Soo, um, what's the rest of the ceremony like?" Finn gives me a grin, "Maybe it should be a surprise." That didn't do anything to stop the butterflies, I think it gave them swords. "Ok, it's just, well, I've never even been to a wedding, I'm just kind of nervous." Finn nods, "I understand sweeting, but don't fret. There's a lot of chanting and a few other things, but it's not terrible, after all, my mother survived it. Unfortunately we lost her due to a poorly healed wound when I was a child. Some kind of blood fever. Sorry, I know that's a bit maudlin for our wedding procession." I give his arm a reassuring squeeze, "I'm sure you miss her." He gives me a sad smile, "I do, very often." We continue on in silence. I start noticing the rocks and the trees, all the varieties that have sprung up over the years. Some have leaves, others have lacy fronds, many have rocks beside them of different shapes and sizes, and now I'm giving myself flashbacks to reading the subsequent books to that one about the dwarves and the short guy. We're finally to the base of the stairs, walking along a wide path to a round area, with a large pile of sticks in the center. Oh holy swiss, they better not be burning me with those sticks. "Absolutely not, we aren't barbarians." I look up to Finn's smiling face, "Sorry, didn't realize that thought happened out loud. I didn't really think so, I'm just a pile of nerves." Finn stops as we approach the pile of sticks, "You can trust me, I knew you would be the perfect avatar of the goddess the moment I spotted you." I look at his smile, and there's something not quite…sane there, and it doesn't reach his eyes. "You see, I need something with a soft figure, good for bearing a son, maybe even more than one. Hopefully you won't get the blood poisoning that my dear mother did." I don't even know what to say at this point, and I really wish I'd made sure the girls were awake. I take a deep breath, maybe it's not as bad, or creepy, as it seems. "What type of blood poisoning?" Maybe if I keep him talking, I can find a way to get loose. "Oh no, I don't want to spoil the fun, I'm sure you'll do much better." The eight women who dressed me followed us into the middle of the circle. They surrounded Finn and I, then I noticed the entire crowd began closing in on us. I gave one last pleading look to Finn, but he was definitely too far gone. The Captain began chanting,

Green Giant
Goddess who saved our ancestors

By the last line, the entire crowd was chanting, screaming, and pushing in. I don't know what they're about to transform me into, but I'm out. The problem, however, is how the heck I'm getting out. "Finn, please, if you truly love me, help me out here." Finn leaned in close, "Sorry dear, it's nothing personal, you were more of a need than a want and you were soooo easy to suck in. The last three women I tried to bring back were impure, wretched whores. Your innocence, however, oozed from your gullible little face from the beginning. I knew you'd be, well, manageable. Now, how about you shut up so we can consummate this thing soon." Ok. I know, tears very rarely do anything to help, but between the hurt and fear, there was a lot of anger, and I couldn't stop it from springing out through my tear ducts. "Oh, look, tears." Finn leaned down and licked the tear from my cheek, "Hmm, salty, can't wait to find out what the rest of you tastes like." The crowd is still pressing in and chanting and I don't see a way out. The women who had painted me green are now holding the metal ropes that are attached to my wrists. They yank my arms, pulling the cords tight. I lost my balance and looked down at the pile of sticks I'd stumbled into. Except they aren't sticks, they're bones. I look up at the statue and it dawns on me how they're going to transform me. They're going to cut off my arms to make me a fitting wife. The fervor of the crowd is almost enough to drown my thoughts. I see the Captain hand Finn a good sized knife. He checks the sharpness and then he turns to me. His face is almost unrecognizable, his freckles, dimples, beautiful eyes, all twisted into an expression of crazed obsession. "Now-now Stacea, be a good little girl and this won't hurt…as much. Don't make me hit anything vital." I close my eyes as he slices into the front of my right shoulder. I hear a shout, but the pain and the stress combine to pull me into unconsciousness.

CHAPTER 17

When I start to come around, my abdomen hurts like it's being punched, I see a lot of blood rolling down my arm, a nice looking butt in black cargo pants, and Flossie. It takes longer than it should to figure out I'm over someone's shoulder and that someone is running, with Floss tailing him. Before I realize what I'm doing, I smack the butt to get the attention of whoever's shoulder is slamming into my abs. "Not now Stace" is that? Surely not, "Oren?" He heaves a sigh, "Yes, but listen, I'm trying to save you right now, can't talk and run that well." I don't even know what to say, so I just dangle, watching Floss and, I have to admit, Oren's butt. We're covering ground fast, and I watch grass go by, "You can put me down, I'm awake now, and this escape may be a little easier." All I get in return is a grunt. "I know I'm heavy." We have reached the dock and he slows down, "I'm going to put you down, but you have to promise not to faint on me." He bends over, bringing his butt closer to my face momentarily as he puts my feet on the ground. I never realized how nice his butt is, but also I'm a bit delirious. He never lets go of me as he straightens back up. "Stace, look at me, we're going to have to jump for the raft I brought over, I was in such a rush to get to you that I didn't tie it correctly." I snicker, yep, still kinda delirious, "Noooo, no way did Inspector Oren Colvin of the space police do something incorrectly." I give him a sarcastic salute, he heaves a sigh and runs a hand down his face, "Listen, you can make fun of me for it the rest of your life, but right now we've got to jump for it and we don't have long before the angry mob catches up to us. If that happens, the rest of your life is going to be a lot shorter." For once in my entire relationship with Oren, I bite my tongue. "Flossie made it over, we'll go together, take my hand." I grab his hand, we run a few steps and leap for the raft. We land in a tangle of arms and legs, Flossie sits on the bench and stares down at us, the little monster. Is that a smirk on her muzzle? I'm trying to untangle all the fabric I'm wrapped in, so I can move. Oren is trying to sit up. Somehow in the process of trying to drag himself up, he's wrapped in part of my dress and I'm more or less tied to his lap. I make eye contact and we both blush, "Ok, I'm ripping some layers off this thing so we can untangle enough to get moving. I think we probably have a lot to discuss, but you're right, we've got to do that later." I yank several layers from my dress, and Oren manages to untangle before I rip off so much it's indecent. I swear Floss is snickering at us. Oren gets the motor started and we begin speeding across the water, not to Ellis Island, but to where the ships are sitting, Oren's single seat ship, and Carol, my giant space bean. I've always loved my ship, but I'm not sure I've ever been so happy to see her as I am now. "Oh Carol, you're a sight for sore eyes." Oren chuckles, "No kidding, running for our lives gives me a new appreciation for her dull red." I smack him lightly on the arm, "Be nice." As we pull up and tie the boat to the old wharf, I freeze. "Wait Oren, my sister, Sher, last I knew they were still sleeping." He climbs the ladder and reaches out a hand, taking my left one and pulling so we don't reopen anything that closed on my right shoulder. "They definitely weren't anywhere on the island when I came back looking for you. Their beds were empty before everyone left for the other Island." There's a sinking feeling in the pit of my stomach. I can't leave without my family. I don't even know where they are, or if they're alright. Oren lays his hand gently on my good shoulder, "Stace, we won't leave them behind, let's get you cleaned up and in something a little more practical and then we'll find them." I place my hand on his, "Thank you Oren, I'm sorry for calling you fake cheese." He smiles, "I probably deserved it, but let's sort through that later, we have to get the girls." Three things happen at once, one, I open the cargo bay to see my sister and best friend bound and gagged, two, Finn reaches the wharf and is busy trying to climb up, and three, Oren shoves me into the cargo bay while he and Flossie charge Finn. I run to Kara and pull her gag out, "Please tell me you didn't marry that motherf-..." before she can finish Sher busts out of her bindings and pulls her gag out, "It doesn't matter Kara, I'll make her a widow." I throw my arms around both of them, "I am so glad to see you both, also, Oren rescued me, there's a long talk in store, but right now, he and Flossie are fighting Finn, I don't think he came alone, and you all are the best backup anyone could have. I'm going to get us ready to take off." They both nod and head out the hatch. I hurry to the controls and get Carol powered up. She's about ready for takeoff as I hear feet run in and the cargo hatch closes. I hit the throttle and we blast through the atmosphere and head for the nearest station. I don't even look back to see how far the crowd made it.

We've got a few hours before we arrive. I look down at myself covered in green green grease paint, dried blood, and what's left of my wedding dress. Now that we're at a safer distance, I need a shower and clothes. I grab soft shorts and a black tank and hit the shower. I don't know what exactly this green stuff is, but it's almost as hard to remove as the dried blood all over me. Once I'm clean, I run a brush through my hair, pull on my clothes, and head out toward the common area. Sheridan is making coffee, Kara is rubbing what looks a lot like blood off of her halberd. Flossie is curled up on Oren's lap and he's petting her. He jumps up, earning a hiss from Floss for dropping her. "You are in much better shape than the last time I saw you, your arm looks like it isn't as bad as I thought." I nod and plop down on the sofa next to the seat he'd abandoned. Kara leans her weapon in the corner and discretely grabs Sheridan and pulls her toward a bunk, giving me a wink. "So, where do we even start?" He sits next to me and begins inspecting my shoulder, "I tried to hail you, when you wouldn't answer I sent you a message, I guess you didn't get it?" I roll my eyes, "I got it alright, you were coming after me, you'll find me, I won't get away from you, there's no escape from justice." Oren looked confused, and then like something had hit him, "Oh no, did it not all come through?" I look him dead in the eye, maybe it hadn't been what I thought. "What was it supposed to say?" Oren cleared his, "Stacea, I'm hoping this will find you in time, I'm afraid if you go to the Village you won't get away, there will be no escape from their trap." Oh my mozzarella, I..was…he..tried, well crap. "Oren I am so sorry, it blew out of my hand before I got a good look at it. I thought you were threatening to arrest me or something." Oren hung his head, "I'm sorry I've definitely gone about everything all wrong. I hate that when I was trying to protect you, your first thought was that I was threatening you. I hate that I've harassed you, although, I promise most of my following you on this run has been to protect you. I know you have no reason to believe me." I look at him, in civilian clothes, with messy hair, and I can definitely forgive him, but I'm holding out for an explanation before I do, "Ok, start from the beginning. I'll listen." He sat up straight and turned to face me, "The beginning is maybe the worst part. I had something of a crush on you since our school days. Unfortunately, my juvenile brain turned everything into competition. When we got older and moved into overlapping careers, I'm ashamed to say, I let my immature reaction continue. I just wanted to maintain contact with you. I know it was selfish, wrong, mean, and kind of creepy. Honestly I enjoy pushing your buttons a little, but I've gone about everything wrong." I was shocked, not only had he carried a torch for me, but he just apologized multiple times. "Go on, there's more to the rest of the story." He clears his throat, "Yes, well, I had seen Finn Nivalia lurking for a while, trying to book passage for his mystery cargo. His appearance and whole schtick reminded me of a couple of missing pilots from prior years. The more I dug, the more I found, but I didn't have quite enough to move on him. When he booked your company, I was doubly motivated to crack the case." Well, I feel like a moron, I can't believe I got suckered in. "Stacea, you are far from being a moron."

"I said that out loud, didn't I?"

"You did. But listen, he's a predator. He has experience working his marks."

"So, the weird religious stuff, um, is that legit?"

"I think so. I think he has probably taken at least a couple of women home to daddy, and they haven't survived the wedding."

"I can see why."

"I did some digging further back and found a few more disappearances every 20 years or so. So this has been going on for a long time."

"I literally stepped on the bones of dozens of missing women." I put my face in my hands and sob. It's all finally hitting me how close I cam to being either murdered or dismembered by someone who had deceived me into believing he loved me. How could I have been so stupid?

"You're, uh, thinking out loud again."

"Sorry."

"No, you have nothing to apologize for, you aren't stupid, and you're safe now." I can't help myself, I scoot closer and lean into him, and he wraps his arms around me. I would not have thought in a million years that one day I'd feel safe and at home in the arms of my childhood rival and my adult nemesis. Or that my face would've oozed all over the poor guy's shirt, although he hasn't noticed that part yet. Flossie joins the pile and starts purring, of course the darn cat-fox had been right all along about the two men. I should definitely listen to her gut rather than my own from now on. I hear a shuffle and a giggle, so I sit up, I wipe at the wet spot on Oren's shirt,not that it helps, "Sorry about the puddle on your shirt, Girls! Just get in here." Kara and Sheridan's faces appear around the corner, "We didn't mean to intrude." I roll my eyes,

"We have GOT to talk about that creepy unison thing." They both laughed, I bet they do it on purpose. "Anyway, Oren has just filled me in on the whole Finn situation, and I have an idea, Oren you probably aren't going to like this, but I say we use me as bait." Oren opened his mouth to object and I put a hand up, "I'll contact the planet, act like I don't remember all the crazy crap that went down, I'll act like I believe Oren kidnapped all of us. What do you guys remember about winding up on the ship?"

"Pretty much nothing, we fell asleep in bed and woke up tied up on the ship." Kara nods her agreement. "Perfect, that fits right in with my story." Oren gives me a questioning look, "What story?" I sit up straighter. "Let me lay it all out…"

CHAPTER 18

By the time Carol reaches the space station, we've set our trap. I sent Finn a message telling him I don't remember what happened during the wedding, but when I regained consciousness I found out we'd all been kidnapped by Oren in my ship, and that he has pretty much lost his mind trying to pin something on me. I told him that I managed to escape from Oren and that I miss him terribly. My ship is locked down, so I can't escape on my own. I asked him to use Oren's ship to fly to this station, and meet me by the waterfall in the park. I had to give him a crash course in, well, not crashing, but fortunately docking can be turned over to a station's virtual interface. I told him the park was a safe place to meet because Sheridan had taken Oren to face the local judicial branch. So I pretty much offered myself up on a silver platter. Honestly, I wasn't sure I was valuable enough to get him to waste his time. Oren told me never to say that again, that I am priceless and Finn is a grade A poop weasel. I, well, I didn't even know how to respond to that. So, now I wait, fortunately with Kara and Sher not far off, which means I'm as safe as I can be. Oren and I had said our goodbyes, which were very different this time. No threats, no harsh words, well, at least none directed at me. I almost felt sorry for Finn, but only almost, the Bleu d'Auvergne. Finn should be here any…well, speak of the shelf stable cheese product, here he comes, looking for all the world like he's happy to see me. I'm wearing the little black dress I never got to use, it's got some assorted ruffles that made hiding a recording device very easy. Finn approaches me, looking more like he did the day we met and less like he did the last time I saw him, maybe fortunately? His face changing is a moment I will never forget. I'm never gonna forget him licking my cheek either, that was gross. Gross, and disturbing. Now, to waggle the bait and spring the trap. Not a literal waggle though, that would be weird.

"Hello! I'm glad you managed to get here!" I smile, even as I feel stomach acid creeping up the back of my throat. This might be my worst idea ever. "Fortunately, that dastardly Inspector left his ship behind. Because transport is hard to come by."
"Speaking of, I believe he's been permanently grounded. Apparently the Coalition doesn't take kindly to kidnapping, stalking, murder...several things."
"Wait, murder? Who did he murder?"
"I'm an only child now, although, does it really count if I'm an orphan?"
"Oh no, my little lady is all alone."
"Well, not entirely. I have you."
"Yes, of course you do, I wouldn't ever let you go." He places his hands on my shoulders and it's all I can do not to gag.
"Oh Finn, it's so good to see you, when I was kidnapped I thought... I thought I'd lost you forever.I just didn't know what I'd do without you."
"Unfortunately you missed the best part of the wedding."
"Yes, I don't remember much about our wedding past being painted green. Did we finish the ceremony? Also, did Oren cut me? I woke up with a stab wound and a long slash. I don't remember when it happened."
"I'm afraid we didn't finish the ceremony. I don't remember you being cut, it must have happened after he took you. I am certainly would never do such a thing to you, Stacea my love."
"Of course it must have been Oren, I never thought he would go so far, it was like he became someone else before my eyes."
"But, sweeting, you're with me now and safe, would you like to come back home with me? We can finish the wedding, you will be my queen for as long as you survive."
"Survive?"
"Did I say survive? I doubt it, for as long as you live."

"Of course, but I do have a couple more questions for you before we head that way."

"Ok? Go on. I will tell you what I can."

"Am I the first bride you've had?"

"I'm not sure why that matters, Dove, I chose you."

"Of course Finn, I just wondered. I can't help but be curious. We got close very quickly, but we didn't really discuss your past."

"I understand, dear. Anything else?"

"One more thing, before we go. I need to tell you something."

"Of course, dear. Anything. I'm so glad you've decided to return to me."

"I have an excellent memory."

"Excuse me?"

"I know everything you did down to the last detail, you creep."

"Wha-..."

"Yep, the yelling, the cutting, the licking a tear from my cheek, every moment-..."

"Listen here you little bitch, you would never have been worthy. You should have stayed and died like the others, like my mother, my grandmother, and her grandmother before that. You are weak, squishy, and honestly, you aren't even pretty, you just have child bearing hips. I should've chosen your sister, she's prettier, taller, thinner, and stronger."

My response was to punch Finn in the face. "Take that you mother-fluffing fluff!" By some great good fortune, I managed to knock him out. I'm literally zero use in a fight, but I'd had enough. I give his prone form one good kick before calling for everyone standing by, "Ok, you guys, you can come out now! Sorry I took the fun out of it for you all, I just couldn't stand his droning on." Kara and Sheridan are the first to reach me. Kara throws her arms around me, "Stace you are beautiful, I can't believe he said all of that to you about me. You're far prettier than I am, and smart, and he was just awful." I push my sister back so she can see my eyes when I answer her, "Kara, we can both be beautiful, and still look nothing alike. Don't worry that he hurt me with that. It wasn't the worst thing he said or did, but regardless, I am FINE. Well, almost, my hand hurts really bad." Kara hugs me again, and Sheridan joins, "We'll get you an ice pack, way to shut him up Stace." The red-headed officer, the one who had actually been assigned to take the report about the bandits, arrives. Oren is right on her heels, as soon as he reaches us, he wraps his arms around me and pulls me close, "I am so proud of you, he's going to have a nice shiner from that punch. I was beside myself" Sheridan slaps me on the back, "I knew you had it in you, you just had to find it." I turn from Oren but stay close, "I just got so mad, I needed him to Stop. Talking." The other officer signals two uniformed women over and they see to it Finn is cuffed and they drag him away. "Thank you Miss Thrush, I'm hoping this weasel sings like a song bird, because I think he might be able to close several missing persons cases for us. Also, Inspector Colvin, you are hereby reinstated from forced leave, however, we are granting you a month's paid leave and your choice of assignment when you return. I'd use it wisely." She looks at Oren and then at me, with a significant glance. "I'm sorry, I've talked to you multiple times now and have missed your name." She nods, "Yes ma'am, it's Officer Parasinni, I hope you stay far from trouble, at least for a while." With that she leaves us, following where the guards had taken Finn. The rest of us head for Carol, Oren at my side , the girls behind us. "So, a month's paid leave and your choice of assignment, where will you go?"

"About that, I know that I've been a pain, a creep, and definitely a nuisance, but, could I spend it with you? I'll clean Flossie's litter, scrub the floors, whatever you'd like"

"Yeah, you definitely have been a nuisance."

"I'm sorry."

"I know."

"I understand."

"I don't think you do." I stop, pull him toward me, and kiss him square on the lips. He freezes for a moment before returning the kiss. We may have antagonized each other for years, but somehow the type of fireworks have changed.

"Well, that was unexpected."

"Should I warn you next time?"

"You don't have to."
So I kissed him again, and this time it lasted even longer. Sheridan and Kara pass us, continuing on toward the ship.

CHAPTER 19

Back on the ship, we discuss where we'd like to go, Oren was invited along of course, and we settle on heading back to Arkensane. "Ok, Oren, you've got bunk options since Kara and Sheridan are taking mine to share. I'm taking the bunk Finn was in, now that I've sanitized the life out of it down to the molecular level." Oren scratches his chin… "Which one is closer to yours?" I blush, "Kara's I think." He grins, "Kara's it is. If you ladies will excuse me, I am going to settle in." He heads down the short hallway carrying his duffle bag, Kara turns to me, "Did you break him? He hasn't yelled at you once?!" I smile, "He's softer on the inside, and he has been around so long he feels like a permanent fixture." They both look at me, and I don't know what they're going to do, but I know it's about to come out in perfect unison. "We're happy for both of you. Plus Flossie likes him." I sigh, "You guys need to stop doing that." They both cackle and take off. Flossie comes over to me and winds around my legs, I lean down to pet her, "I know girly, I know. I should've listened to you." She lets out a weird warble, and scampers off. I head to the console and set the controls for a direct jump to Arkensane. Maybe we can pick up a run from there as well. Might as well pick up a little business if I can. Oren comes and stands next to me. "'I've always liked your ship, even though she looks like a bean." I lean into his arm, "Me too. Carol is as much a part of my family as Flossie is." We stand in companionable silence, watching the heavenly bodies go by. I turn slightly toward Oren, "You know you're welcome to stay on as long as you'd like. I can always use an extra pair of hands." Oren takes my hands, "I think I'd like that, although I do have another commission I'm seriously considering though." I nod and he continues, "There's a post that would only require me to be there four months out of the year." That's unusual, "Why? Where?" He continues, "It's on Yooran, they station someone there during the season, townhouse, wardrobe, everything. Plus, I can take a companion along. I know this is kind of sudden, but would you consider, um, being my companion?" He's literally offering me something I could not resist. I want so badly to leave him in a little suspense, but I just can't hide my excitement. "Oren, absolutely, there's no way I could turn that down. But, I have a condition." He smiles, "Anything, if I can make it happen, I will. Just please don't tell me you want to join me as a sister." I laugh, "I'm going to need a mustard gown to match your suit, and you're going to need a puce suit." He runs a hand down his face, "You're serious, aren't you? Are you sure?"

"Absolutely, I'm sure about both. Then we can look ridiculous together."

"Both outfits?"

"The outfits and the company."

"Oh, good. For a moment I was scared"

"Sorry about that, I didn-...Holy swiss!"

"What is it? Please don't tell me you've changed your mind."

"The crate."

"What crate?"

"Finn's crate, it was never unloaded and I absolutely need to know what's in it. Come on"

"Um, are you certain? What if it's dangerous."

"Definitely. It passed several security scans,the documents were legit too."

"Ok, but let's wait until we dock and open it someplace safe, just in case."

"Ok, I guess. It's going to be really hard to wait."

Sheridan and Kara scamper into the domed bridge, "What's the excitement about?Are you two-..." I turn to her, "The crate. We still have it. I need to know what's in it, or I will just die. Come on." I lead the way into the cargo hold. We all stare at the crate, frozen. Kara breaks the silence first, "I can smash it open." Oren looks over at her, "Um, are you sure?" Kara shrugs, "Yup, or pry it with one of my polearms." Oren lets out a low whistle, "Remind me to never cross her." I laugh, but Sheridan answers him, "My lady is incredibly strong, and I'm one of the best shots in the galaxy, just remember that if you ever consider hurting Stacea. She would never retaliate, Kara and I aren't so nice." Oren, slightly paler than a moment ago, gulps, I roll my eyes, "Guys, seriously can we focus on the matter at hand?" I start looking over the crate, there's a keypad in a little indent on the side, I don't have the code, but if it pry it off...it falls into my hand and I look at the back, yep, just as I thought. "Somebody grab me a screwdriver." I stick my hand out and a screwdriver lands in my palm, I jam it into the small opening on the back and wiggle it, prying the back of the keypad open. I find exactly what I was looking for, a little red button, I press and hold it and the octothorpe until the lights flash in the numbers on the keypad. One, three, five, and...seven. I turn the keypad over, press in the code, and there's a hiss as the airtight container pops open. I step back to join the others, we all stare at the giant crate in silence. "Are we ready? I know we were going to wait, I just... I mean...we got it open, so why not look?" Kara and Sheridan shrug...in unison...again. "You two are creeping me out, you have got to stop." Oren puts a hand on my arm, "Step back Stace, let me open it, just in case, I want you safe." I let him step in front of me, "Ok, but I'm right here, you be careful." I place my hand over his, this is very new, but it feels...safe. He reaches for the door and slowly pulls it open. Nothing happens, and we all stand there, staring into the crate. Of all the things I could've imagined, this... was not it.

"Seriously?"

"I can't even..."

"No wonder it passed the scans."

"Every flip-flopping thing we went through, the lies, the manipulation, the travels, although it was a nice trip, almost marrying that rat's butthole, and getting freaking stabbed all because of this?!?!?! No. No. No-no-no. It seriously cannot freaking be this."

I step forward and feel around to make sure, not false sides or bottom, no hidden panels. Lying on the floor of the very large crate, is one single item. It's not even a plant, it's...it's....a tiny carved bust...of William Shakespeare? I pick it up, it's not even plaster or stone, it's rubber? Or something similar. I search around the sides and bottom, maybe there's a hidden compartment? As I turn it over in my hands I notice the base twists, maybe it opens? I twist it a little further and the neck extends and starts vibrating. Oh no. I throw it back into the crate and slam the door. "If that's what I think it is, I'm going to hurl." Sheridan bursts into laughter so hard she's hanging from Kara's arm, Kara is trying to hold her up while tears fall from her eyes while laughing, "I don't know what's funnier, the whole situation, or your reaction to it." I turn to look at Oren, who is doing his very best to not to laugh. "Ok, ok, it's a little funny." Oren's snicker finally escapes his tightly closed mouth, and I join him. Once we all regain our composure, I turn to everyone, "Now that we've handled that, I'll cook dinner, I'm feeling stir fry." With that I head up the stairs to the kitchen and get to work. Oren joins me and it's ready in a jiffy. After dinner, the girls clean up. I grab my book and head for the couch, Oren joins me, "So, you have quite a library, I've always regretted that living in the Coalition barracks never gave me the space for one. I could only check out a couple of books at a time." I patted the spot next to me, "You're definitely welcome to mine, and we can swap out for anything you'd like." Oren picked up a book and sat next to me, "You have an excellent selection. I've never read this one." I look over, he's picked a near ancient thriller, about a man who lived beneath an opera house, and an ingenue. I lean lightly against his arms, and Floss hops on the couch. She curls up in between us, resting her head on Oren's lap. We sit and read in companionable silence as Carol speeds toward Arkensane.

I wake up to the smell of pancakes and coffee, my pillow is... breathing? I open my eyes and realize I must've fallen asleep leaning on Oren as we read together. Now my head is against his chest and his arm is around me. I could get used to this. I sit up and try not to disturb Oren as I stand and stretch. I walk in the kitchen, Kara and Sheridan are making breakfast. I head to the console and check our location, we're a couple of hours out from Arkensane. I head back to the table, I guess I woke Oren, he's there too. "Good morning! Sorry I fell asleep on you, literally." He puts his arm around me, "It was nice. Do not apologize." He kisses me on the head, I could really get used to this. "Good, because I could too." I have got to stop thinking out loud. "I find it endearing." I turn to him, "Great, because apparently it's not going away."

A few days later, Oren and I are lounging in a moderately warm pool, sipping on some sort of punch in a fishbowl. "So, about the alpaca incident…"
Oren turns to face me, "Yes?"
I turn on my seat to face him,
"I only copied you because your idea was much better than mine."
"Stace, you really don-…"
"I do. Listen, I was going to make a diorama of an oil spill, but it was going to be so plain and then I found out what you were doing and, well, alpacas are cuter than poor baby seals covered in oil. I really did feel bad, but you were so mean about it."
"Stace, I only ever brought it up because it was my excuse to talk to you, like I said, my behavior was terrible and I did everything the wrong way."
"Oren, I understand, but I was in the wrong too. I want us to start whatever this becomes on a level playing field. With everything out in the open."
"I can respect that, and this can be whatever you want it to be. I know how I've always felt, but I also know I created negative interactions."
"You certainly did, but I helped feed them, too."
"Only because I picked at you."
"I'll give you that one."
We both settle back into our seats, watching the moons dip below the horizon, it's peaceful and there aren't many people here, it almost feels like it's just us.

"Stace?"

"Yeah?"

"Can I say something?"

"Sure."

"I love you."

"Oren..."

"It's ok"

"But Or-..."

"You don't have to say it back, truly."

"B-.."

"I just needed to tell you"

"Oren!" I slap my hand across his mouth before he can say anything else, "Oren you are going to shut up and listen to me, do you understand?" He mumbles something from beneath my hand, I put my other finger to my lips to shush him. He has the sheer audacity to lick my hand. It startles me enough to make me pull my hand back, "Hey, none of that, and you still better hush up." Oren is laughing out loud so hard he can't talk and is starting to gasp for air when Kara and Sher swim up, "Is he ok?" the unison persists. "You two are going to give me nightmares." Now they're cackling and Oren has about pulled himself together, "St..ha... Stace...really, it's fine, we have all the time in the world." I don't know whether to scream, cry, or laugh myself, I'm so flustered. I settle on diving into the deeper water and I swim away from the whole pack of hyenas. When I surface, I'm several feet away. That'll teach Oren to stop me when I'm trying to tell him I love him too. I look for the ladder on this side of the pool and swim toward it. I get up the first couple of steps before I realize someone is standing right at the ladder. Look up to see Finn's father glaring down at me. This is bad, this is really, really bad. Captain Nivalia reaches down and grabs my arm, dragging me out of the water. He pulls me at a pace that makes me nearly have to jog to keep up. I finally manage to scream, but I'm cut off quickly. He produces a knife and jabs it into my ribs. I wince, he broke skin, but the cut isn't deep. I do notice after a few minutes part of my bathing suit is a deeper red and there's redding water sliding down the outside of my leg. I know I should keep my mouth shut, but I really just can't. "Why in the name of soft nutty camembert do you Nivalia men keep ducking stabbing me?!?!" He turns and moves his grip to my throat, "You have blasphemed against the Goddess, none escape, hideous wretch. They die or they bear sons, or bear sons and then die. That is the purpose of the brides we find. Ignorant, lowly, self-conscious worms like you are easy to charm. You took my son from me, you will bear me a new one or you will perish from the attempts. Then perhaps I'll take your fairer sister, or the little brown one, although she seems a bit feisty for my tastes." At this point, he has me pinned to a tree with his hand around my throat, his body pressing ever closer. I can't help it, if I go down, it will be fighting. "Listen you hateful bastard, I will die before I help you continue your twisted family. If that means I die, then so be it. But if you touch my sister or my friend? I will find a way to kill you from beyond the grave, and when you enter the afterlife, I will be first in line to torture your worthless soul." I was about to spit in his face when it disappeared. I fell to the ground and looked up to see Oren slam the Captain to the ground. Kara and Sher arrived in time to add a couple solid stomps to him before Flossie, who I thought was on the ship, tears his throat out. "Well, that was messy." Oren is by my side in a flash, "Come here Stace, I am so sorry, I didn't see him sooner, are you ok? Why the hell are you bleeding? Can I kill him again?" He gathers me on to his lap and I see tears forming in his eyes. "Oren, I love you. I was scared I would die before I had a chance to say it. But I mean it." I wrap my arms around him and let myself do something I rarely do, especially more than once, sob into his shoulder. Coalition officers arrive and Sheridan and Kara fill them in on who is who and what happened. Fortunately, all the loose ends were tied up quickly and we were allowed to go back to the ship. I went and showered and put on comfy clothes. Floss curled up next to me on the couch, until Oren joined me. "Stace, I've almost lost you twice, you better be used to me dogging every step, because I am NEVER letting you get hurt again." I lean into him and sigh, "I ought to be by now, huh? I'm definitely ok with it, I like having you around. I'm also incredibly excited about spending the season on Yooran every year. If I didn't love you for anything else, I'd love you for that." Oren holds me tighter, "I look forward to it, even if you insist on matching mustard formal clothing." I chuckle, "I do insist." Oren holds me until I drift off to sleep.

CHAPTER 20

The white cathedral in Yooran's capital city is decorated in white flowers with gold ribbons. I walk down the aisle behind the ring bearer and the, somewhat unusual, flower girl. My feet crush the strewn flowers, releasing a pleasant scent as I walk down the aisle. I turn and catch Oren's eye and wink, he slips his hand into mine as we stand at the altar. Then music begins as the two bride's enter, did you think this was my wedding? Silly reader, no. I am the only bridesmaid, and my dear Oren is the flower girl, with Floss as the ringbearer. We stand witness to my sister and best friend's nuptials, and we are throwing them a ball this evening in lieu of a reception. As they exchange vows, I look on, holding Oren's hand. Maybe one day it will be our turn, but not just yet. As they kiss at the close of the ceremony and leave, we follow them out.

At the reception, I spend every waltz in Oren's arms. "You know the one drawback of marrying me will be that it's against custom for spouses to dance with each other here." I laugh at Oren, "What do you mean marrying you? You haven't asked." Oren grins, "Not yet." I pull him off to the side, into an alcove in our ballroom. "You cannot ask me to marry you at someone else's wedding, Kara might not care, but Sheridan will skin you alive." Oren chuckles, "I know for a fact Sher won't mind."
"Have you met Sheridan?"
"Yes, before I met you."
"She will not be happy if you do what I think you are about to do…"
"She told me to…"
Just then, two women in white gowns smash into our tiny alcove, Sheridan looks at Oren, "Well, have you done it yet?" Oren throws

a glance at me, "She thinks you'll kill me." Sheridan looks at me, "I will not, I told him to."
"Oh"
"So Stace, now that you are assured of my safety, will you marry me?"
"I have conditions, no green paint, no slicing or stabbing, and no chanting."
"Absolutely." As I throw myself into his arms, "In that case, yes, Oren, I will definitely marry you."